S. Webb.

Nov 45.

(paguined ed.

(2n ed 5)

STRANGE GLORY

BY L. H. MYERS

(485)

D1392315

Owing to wartime production difficulties it is impossible to maintain large stocks of our publications and the titles available change so rapidly that the issuing of a catalogue would be of little value as a guide to intending purchasers. Readers wishing to be informed of books now in print will be sent a list on receipt of a penny stamp or a stamped and addressed envelope.

STRANGE GLORY

BY

L. H. MYERS

PENGUIN BOOKS

HARMONDSWORTH MIDDLESEX ENGLAND
245 FIFTH AVENUE NEW YORK U.S.A.

First published February 1936
Reprinted March 1936
Reprinted May 1936
Published in Penguin Books 1945

TO

PAULINA

MADE AND PRINTED IN GREAT BRITAIN FOR PENGUIN BOOKS LIMITED,
BY RICHARD CLAY AND COMPANY, LTD., BUNGAY, SUFFOLK

A Stranger here
Strange things doth meet, strange Glory see;
Strange Treasures lodg'd in this fair World appear,
Strange all and new to me:
But that they mine should be who Nothing was,
That strangest is of all; yet brought to pass.

THOMAS TRAHERNE

STRANGE GLORY

PART I

I

SUDDENLY she leaned forward and told the driver to stop. After getting out she stood for a minute hesitant, looking down the rough track that melted away into the forest. She said: "Wait for me, please," and the chauffeur, an old man, smiled benignly, for she was a very elegant young lady, and a stranger —English, most likely. He would have liked to tell her all sorts of things about the country, only she looked so very dreamy and at the same time so concentrated. Concentrated on what? He couldn't imagine.

She began to walk slowly down the track, and he saw her staring about eagerly, not minding when the ruts made her stumble. She would be about twenty, he supposed. Probably this was her first visit to Louisiana—or to America for that matter. How slender she was, and how pretty in that soft grey dress! Presently at a bend in the road she disappeared. He looked up into the sky and yawned.

Paulina, too, looked up into the sky. It was mild and distant; a gentle sky, she thought. The air, too, was mild—and soft and damp, and faintly smelling of swamp. On each side of the track were dry weeds, and big tufts of a coarse silvery grass, and dwarf palmettos that made the scene tropical. And how still it was! how still after Pontchartrain! She stopped to listen to the stillness; she held her breath.

"Now I am all alone," she said to herself. "All alone in a Louisiana swamp! This is a part of the great swamp-forest, and down there is the Gulf."

Yielding to a sudden impulse, she left the track and made her way towards a fringe of trees. These trees were tall and gaunt, already half killed by the grey moss that hung in beards from every branch. Grey moss—Spanish moss it was called. Drearily, drearily it hung in the windless air. It was like old age. And whole forests were dying from it. Dying forests!

Windless   air!   Grey-bearded   age!   And   silence—always
silence!

She stood still and listened again.   The faint, the very faint,
hum of an occasional mosquito was the only sound she could
hear.   Overhead faint grey clouds were floating at an immense
height; in the west the sun was faintly visible through the brown
forest blur.   Sometimes, thought Paulina, sometimes there must
be winds to shake these old grey beards.   And oh, how melancholy mad the trees would then look!   A forest of King Lears!
with the wind whistling through their long grey beards.   Sad!
Sad and ridiculous!

Again she moved forward, but cautiously, for the spiky
palmettos were pricking her calves.   The soil was spongy, and
when her heel broke through the surface a stronger smell of
swamp came up to her.   She was right under the trees now;
and some that were white like skeletons bore upon their trunks
a delicate tracery of scarlet lichen.   She scratched the lichen
with her finger, and the scratching made a great noise in the
silence; and when she moved forward again the rustle of her
feet among the fallen leaves embarrassed her by its loudness.
"This is a place," she thought, "for only ghosts to move in."
But wasn't she, in her grey dress, very nearly a ghost?   Didn't
she feel empty enough, bodiless enough, vague and distant and
melancholy enough, to be one?   She smiled a little, for it pleased
her to think so.

The sun by this time had dipped beneath the horizon and only
a faint light was coming through the brushwood, a rusty glow
that lost itself in the dusk spread by the grey-bearded trees.
Paulina shivered, partly because her dress was very thin, and
partly because she suddenly felt afraid.   "But I should hear
anyone coming," she said to herself.   "No one could come
within half a mile without my hearing him."   No, but someone
might be there already; a pair of eyes might be watching her;
someone might be standing quite motionless in the undergrowth,
and. . . . For a moment her heart stood still; then almost
equally suddenly she lost all sense of alarm.   A man *was* watching her.   He was sitting on a fallen tree-trunk not more than
twenty yards away.   His attitude was one of meditation; and,
if his eyes were fixed on her, it was in a stare that was reassuringly
speculative and remote.   For a few moments, involuntarily, she
stared back, then turned her head away.   The man was quite
old—nearly fifty, she thought; and he looked like a gentleman.

Drawing herself up with a purposeful air, she turned and

began to walk back. But she had not taken more than a few steps before the man got up—she saw this out of the corner of her eye—and moved towards her. At once her heart began to beat faster, but she controlled herself and preserved an air of detachment and unconcern. As he came up the stranger said: " You're going the wrong way, I think."

" Oh."

" You want to get to the road, don't you?"

" Yes."

" Then that's the way you should go." And he pointed.

" Oh—thank you."

They exchanged polite smiles, and she changed her direction.

. . . . .

The car ran gently along the smooth road in the dusk, and Paulina was rocked into a dream. This lasted until the big cemetery was reached, and then—as on the way out—she stared in fascination. On the other side of the canal that bordered the road there was a line of weeping-willows, and behind these were tombs of white marble, one and all shaped like large dog-kennels. Hundreds and hundreds of them were scattered among the ilexes and cypresses of this vast cemetery. It was odd, she thought, but there was something beautiful as well as absurd in the spectacle they presented. In answer to her questions the chauffeur had explained that the bodies of the dead couldn't be put underground because as soon as you turned up a sod you came to water. But what did that matter? Would she, when her time came, prefer to be put into a dog-kennel? Perhaps, when one was old, one's ideas changed.

And then her mind went back to the man who had spoken to her in the wood. Did he, when he drove past this place, imagine himself here? Had he already chosen a little white-marble house for himself? And did he find the thought of it depressing?

Now the car was turning into a wide boulevard that ran right into the heart of the town. In front of her, cliff-like against the darkening sky, there rose the tall, modern buildings of Pontchartrain. Their black masses geometrically pricked out with clusters of lighted windows, their summits twinkling with illuminated signs, they made a splendid and complicated pattern in mid air. As the car sped forward ribbons of red, yellow, green, and steely blue light multiplied themselves all round her; the air, which had been cool and damp near the cemetery, now became urban and was filled with the noises of town life.

Paulina, who was still deep in her dreams, noticed very little
of this; in a dream she got out when the car drew up before her
hotel; in a dream she passed in through the revolving door;
and still in a dream moved through the hot, tobacco-thickened
air of the long, crowded hall. As a rule she was uncomfortably
aware of the stares that were fastened upon her as she passed;
she was made conscious of her figure, of her clothes, of everything. But this evening, although as many eyes as ever were
fixed upon her, her own eyes, very wide-open, very blue, very
childlike in their gaze, saw nothing. A slender grey ghost, she
moved swiftly and smoothly along past the stalls and stands and
office-counters to the gilded bank of lifts. Automatically she
entered one, and automatically got out at the sixteenth floor.
Automatically she walked down the dim tunnel-like passage,
the thick carpet muffling her tread, the hot stale air catching at
her throat. On arriving at the door of her room, she found
she had no key: that meant going through the sitting-room, in
which—she could hear their voices—her mother and aunt were
holding one of their endless colloquies. She went in.

" Darling, how late you are! Was it a good film? "

" A good film? . . . Oh, yes, not bad."

" What was it about? "

" Oh—people—rather silly people. But it was so hot, terribly
hot. I simply must have a bath."

She slipped into her bedroom, shut the door, and went to
the open window—without turning on the light. Pontchartrain,
wrapped in a warm misty Louisiana night, lay beneath her.
How strange America was! But for the feel of the air this
might almost have been New York. . . . Everywhere the same
buildings and streets and noises and lights. . . .

Ah! Suddenly she stiffened and drew in her breath. There
it was again—that ridiculous, unearthly sound! It was a music
that seemed to have no one place of origin but to pervade in the
same moment of time every region of the night. It was a thin,
sharp, penetrating whine, and she now knew it to come from
the pleasure-boat on the river. The steam from its boilers
operated some monstrous musical apparatus that sent this vulgar
and yet unearthly whine quivering through the air. Not loud,
not full, but ubiquitous and infinitely penetrating, it was a call
to pleasure—a call to all those young men and girls who were
now streaming through the busy streets.

Paulina shivered. A week ago, on the evening of her arrival,
at a moment when memory was plunging her into the throes of

a more than usually devastating access of love, these needle-like strains had for the first time stabbed her ears. Rupert! Oh, Rupert! This music and Rupert were now identified. Where was Rupert at this moment? What doing? What thinking? Was he thinking of *her*? Oh, Rupert!

Suddenly she spun round, ran to the switch and turned on all the lights. She shut the window with a bang, drew the curtains and brushed the back of her hand rapidly over her eyes. " Damn Rupert! " she said, and began to undress.

Kicking off her shoes, she dragged her grey dress with savage roughness over her head, and rapidly hurled her other garments from her. Naked she went into the bathroom and turned on the taps, then came back to examine her figure in the wardrobe glass. It was a very nice figure—in fact, it was lovely. Satisfied, she picked up a book of poetry and stretched herself out in the warm water for a quarter of an hour's perfect bliss.

II

A YEAR passed, and Paulina was again in Pontchartrain. At nightfall, on the day of her arrival, she was again standing in the window of the same room, looking down upon the lights and illuminated signs that she remembered well. Almost immediately in front of her, but a quarter of a mile away, there was an enormous hand that filled a glass with a ruby liquor, then vanished, then filled the glass with an amber liquor, then vanished again. Paulina gazed at it in deep meditation.

Time—how mysterious! During each one of the many nights that she had been away that hand had silently and unremittingly replenished that glass! All night and every night, while she had been on the ocean, and in Paris and 'in Athens, that quiet persistent tempting of the inhabitants of Pontchartrain had gone on. Had many of them turned drunkards in consequence?

" Just a year ago, and I am just one year older! " She gave a sigh that was half satisfaction and half regret. What a lot had happened to her in twelve months! How much she had changed!

But here nothing had changed—or so it seemed. The same damp warm atmosphere enveloped the town; the same dry stale air suffocated her as she walked along the passage; the soap in her bathroom had the same smell; and the same business

men, the same girls behind the counters, the same glare and
smoke and noise made the long hall below just what it had
always been.

And now she was waiting for the music. She felt that if it
came—if suddenly, mysteriously, those needle-like notes took
possession of the night—she would shiver, she would have
gooseflesh, she would burst into tears. Plangent, plangent,
plangent—that was the word—and how clever of her to find it
upon her tongue! Oh heavens! the music—here it was again!
While she was still smiling, it began.

Immediately she thought of Rupert. Rupert, alas, *had*
suffered change; he had become a ghost and her love of him
was now a shadow. The Rupert and the Paulina of a year ago—
those had vanished! A deep discouragement overcame her.
It seemed to her that she failed in all her undertakings. Her
feelings lacked depth and permanence alike. She could find
nothing in herself to admire.

The music ceased, and, still in the dark, she sat down upon
the bed. " I want enduring things," she thought, " dependable
things. I want dependableness in myself—I don't want only
appearances of sameness—like the smells, and the business men,
and the damp Pontchartrain air.—I want things that are the
same to themselves—persons, I suppose—and I want to be the
same to myself and to them."

And then she thought of the swamp-forest, and of the pattern
of lichen on the tree-trunk. Quite illogically it seemed to her
that she and the swamp-forest would recognize each other as
the same. That bit of forest had occupied her thoughts several
times in the past year, and often she had had a longing to revisit
it. " I will go to-morrow," she said to herself. " I will start
at just the same hour; and everything shall be just the same."

As she thought about it she began to feel excited. Of course,
if it rained, or if the sun were too bright, she would not go.
No: the sky must be pale and lofty; the air must be still; the
tall, dejected, grey-bearded trees must stand motionless; the
faint, faint hum of an occasional mosquito must be the only
sound to be heard. She herself would be wearing a very similar
dress; and she would look at the scarlet lichen, and lay her
hand upon the tree-trunk—all just the same as before.

.   .   .   .   .   .

The next day was favourable and she set out. She was feeling
rather elated, for she had succeeded in tracing the taxi-driver

who had driven her a year ago, and this was particularly fortunate because otherwise she would never have managed to find the place again. But the nice old man remembered her, and, although his replies at first had not been helpful, after an interval of severe meditation, the light of proud self-confidence had illuminated his features.

" I guess I know where I set yer down," he said.

" No! " She was jubilant.

" I guess I know."

" But that's wonderful! "

" I guess I know."

And he was as good as his word. On her way out the first point that she recognized was the cemetery, and again it struck her as both beautiful and ridiculous, and again there came into her mind the thought of the elderly man she had seen under the trees. " Perhaps he's already dead," she said to herself. " Perhaps he is already in one of those dog-kennels."

A quarter of an hour later the car stopped, and there before her, to her great satisfaction, was the rough track with the same ruts, the same tufts of spiky grass, the same palmettos and nondescript little bushes on either side. After walking a few yards she paused. She looked all round, she looked up into the sky, she listened to the deep, deep silence. It might have been a year ago: nothing had changed. Gazing at a small palmetto that was spreading its formal fan out in front of her with a slightly affected grace, she wondered what the year had held for *it* in the way of experience—a great storm of wind, perhaps?—a drought, a flood? And thinking of Paris and Athens, and of Rupert and all her own adventurings—" Which of us has had the better time?" she wondered. " Which has been the better life? "

The forest, when she came to it, seemed to her very beautiful. It gave her the same impression of strangeness as before, and to this there was added an emotion that memory brought. " I shall come here every year," she said to herself. " Just once, not more."

In a muse she wandered on a little further than last time, stopping only when a faint undercurrent of uneasiness ruffled the serenity of her contemplation. This uneasiness was born of the silence, for the silence made her feel, not that she was alone, but that she was being watched. And then—just as before—she became aware that she *was* being watched. The same man was watching her; but this time he was not sitting on a log but leaning against a tree; and this time he was looking at her not with indifference but with interest.

She had given a slight start, upon which the man stirred, and while he came slowly forward she examined him with curiosity. He didn't look like an American; he was probably English, she thought. His long lean figure was clothed in grey home-spun. His hair was grey, his face clean-shaven and much lined. It was a squarish face with eyes set far apart, a straight nose, a long upper lip, and a firm mouth and chin. A rather grim face, but his smile reassured her; it was very pleasant.

"You were here last year," he said. "I recognize you."

She smiled. "Yes. You showed me the way."

And now there was a pause. It was for him to go on, but he showed no consciousness of this, and his continuing smile was so tranquil that she let the silence prolong itself. At last, however, feeling that something was called for—"I liked this place so much," she said, "that I wanted to come again."

"I like it, too," was his reply. He was evidently pleased, but not in the least surprised. And yet why should she come back after a year to visit a spot that had nothing particular to distinguish it? Puzzled, she suddenly asked herself whether he was not a solitary, an eccentric. This idea was lent some support by what he next said.

"If you like I'll show you my house."

"Your house?"

"It's quite near—about a hundred yards from here. In a clearing behind those trees. I'll show you the way."

With this he moved slowly off, and after a moment's hesitation she followed. There was no path, and he slouched along in a desultory manner, skirting round the palmettos and boggy places without once looking back to see if she was coming. It was all rather odd, but after a minute his tranquillity communicated itself to her, and she ceased to wonder. She was able once again to give her attention to the forest, to notice the mosses and grasses that were new to her, to become aware of the waning of the light, the cooling of the air, and the general feel of the closing of the day. He went so slowly that she even had time to halt and examine the scarlet lichen on the tree-trunks and lay her hand upon the cool smooth bark and think: "This is just like last year."

When his house came into view she suffered a disappointment. She had not consciously been expecting anything very romantic, but this shack—there was no other word for it—was quite singularly devoid of charm. In fact it was one of the ugliest, cheapest-looking little houses that she had ever seen—ugly even for America. It was painted chocolate-brown, and, apart from the felling of a few trees, nothing had been done to the rough piece of ground upon which it had been dumped down. But what offended her most was a clothes-line (stretched from one corner to the nearest tree), upon which hung two dish-cloths and three or four pairs of socks. Paulina very much objected to anything ' squalid,' and that clothes-line was undeniably squalid, as was also the litter in front of the house—wood-chips and sawdust, a heap of corn-cobs, bits of sacking, and—worst of all—old tins! Very unattractive, too, were the remains of tea left out upon a wooden table in the veranda.

" Oh, how nice!" she exclaimed, and then in order to add something: " Have you lived here long?"

" A goodish time—in fact for years," replied the man vaguely. He had turned, he was looking at her, and his face showed such pleasure in her company that she made a determined effort to appear enthusiastic. " It's charming," she murmured.

" Oh well!" He clearly was not deceived. " The *place* is beautiful, anyhow. As for the house, it does look rather shabby, I'm afraid." And his eyes dwelt upon it critically.

Paulina was distressed. " I've spoilt it for him," she thought. " This is dreadful." That he should be quick to see what she was thinking, and sensitive to her opinion—these things flattered her. She gave him a warm look. " Oh no!" she said. " I wasn't thinking that."

He returned her gaze humorously and laughed. The friendliness that he detected in her evidently made up to him for her unspoken thoughts. What he said was: " Anyhow, it doesn't really matter. It's a very large forest, and this is a very small house. Besides, no one ever comes here."

Paulina could protest no more; she smiled; but the next moment self-consciousness overtook her, and she began to make conversation. It must be so nice to live by one's self in the forest; not to be running to the telephone all the time; to have plenty of leisure for—for reading, and everything. But it was getting late, and she must go back now. The sun was just setting, and it got dark so quickly.

Her companion's eyes continued to rest on her with a visible pleasure; but she was slightly discomfited to see that he was not listening. " I must go back," she repeated very decisively.

"Oh, must you? This is your way." And he started off in front of her like a guide.

"What was the point of showing me that horrible little house?" She said this to herself in a sudden fit of impatience. "However, he's a nice man all the same." For a while her eyes rested pensively on the tall figure before her, but it was not long before her thoughts left him, and she entered once again into a deep awareness of the forest, which, with the actual setting of the sun, was passing through a moment of change. In the particular coolness, the particular hush, of these minutes the whole vegetable world seemed to be silently altering the rhythm of its life. Paulina sank into a dream, and it was not until they had left the trees behind them and were halfway up the track that she noticed that she and her guide were still keeping their distance, he going some five yards ahead. "This is rather absurd," she thought, and quickened her pace until she had drawn nearly abreast. She was going to make conversation again, but then she noticed that he was as completely abstracted as she had been a moment ago. Quietly she fell back.

When they reached the car he put out his hand to open the door for her, and for a moment, disconcerted, she thought that they were going to part like that. But while she stood with one foot on the running-board, he brought his remote and brooding gaze down to her and his old smile returned—a smile of recognition and pleasure. She returned it with relief, stepped in, and the car drove off.

III

DURING the next few days Paulina's thoughts often went back to the hermit (as she called him to herself) and she resolved to visit him—or, at any rate, his forest—again. But she was equally determined not to tell her mother anything about it; this was not the kind of thing her mother would understand; and a week went by before she managed to slip off.

This time, as the car drew up beside the rough track, she noticed something that had escaped her before—a signboard announcing that the land round about was for sale. She stared at it disconcerted. It stated plainly enough that all this part of the forest, including the ground on which the hermit's house stood, was purchasable in small lots for building purposes.

Paulina got out of the car and moved slowly—very slowly—

down the track. How odd not to have noticed that enormous signboard before! Her bit of swamp-forest (she sometimes thought of it as hers and sometimes as the hermit's) was threatened with devastation. The more she considered it the more distressed she became. Twice she walked up and down the whole length of the track, for she didn't want to meet the hermit until she had cleared her mind. *Why*, she wondered, was she taking this matter so much to heart? What was it that made her feel as she did about this particular piece of land? No satisfactory answer came. The only light she could get sprang out of the recollection that very often in the train, when for some reason or other a halt had been made in open country, she had stared out of the window and thought: " In that particular corner of that field I could find perfect peace. There I could live—like a tuft of grass or a tree—watching the evening and the morning, and the seasons as they come and go—without restlessness, at peace with everything." But of course she really knew quite well that if she *were* to find herself in that field, it would seem to her just like any other field—a damp, uncomfortable place in which one had no wish to linger.

The strange thing was that in this bit of the swamp-forest her feelings were quite different. Here she actually did want to linger—and even to take root. Yes, it had been so on her first visit a year ago; and the same feeling had come back this year. Here that feeling seemed able to realize itself; here it came into being and endured; and, like the forest itself, it couldn't be transplanted.

Then she thought of the hermit. Did he feel as she did about this particular place? She doubted it. If smug little houses were to grow up all round him, he would just move away. He would move, she supposed, to some remoter part of the swamp-forest; and she could imagine him doing it without much regret. She frowned, feeling slightly resentful.

When at last she went on into the forest it was with the determination to have a talk with the hermit about that odious signboard. So she turned her steps boldly in the direction of his house, and was presently rewarded by the sight of him sitting in his veranda, his eyes half closed, a cigarette between his lips, the very picture of contentment and serenity.

As soon as she appeared, however, he sprang to his feet. " How nice to see you! " he called out, and came down the steps to greet her.

Flattered as she did indeed feel by his unmistakable pleasure,

in her heart a strange little flame of indignation was burning.
How could the man be so carefree when his piece of swamp-
forest stood in danger of utter ruin?

" I am going to give you tea," he said, with evident satisfaction
at the prospect.   She didn't want tea, and she didn't expect that
his tea would be at all nice; but it was impossible to refuse, so
she sat in the rocking-chair impatiently rocking herself, while
her host made a clatter inside the house. Tea, however, was
produced quite quickly, and to her surprise it was very good
China tea. In order to say something she told him how exasper-
ated her mother always was when, lifting the lid of the hotel
teapot, a little muslin bag met her eyes. This was the first
mention she had ever made of her circumstances, her daily life;
and now, upon his failing to take advantage of the opening she
had just given him, her impatience increased.

" To-day, for the first time," she said after a pause, " I noticed
the signboard on the road. I—I was horrified."

" A signboard? " His attention was all on the teapot which
he was re-filling. " Oh yes, it has been up for some weeks."

" How long? "

" A good many weeks. I can't exactly remember.—Do have
some more tea."

Paulina suddenly felt quite hysterical. " But—but all this
piece of the forest may be sold at any moment! The trees may
be cut down—to make room for hideous little houses." Her
voice had a quaver in it, and the annoyance this caused her
almost brought tears to her eyes.

The man, who was still bending over the tea-table, glanced up
quickly, and a look of surprise came into his face.

" No, that shan't happen." This, after a brief pause, was said
in a tone that had changed completely. " You needn't worry,"
he added.

There was a silence, during which Paulina surveyed herself
with no little astonishment. " I am quite ridiculous," she
thought.

The man handed her the jam. " You are right," he went on.
" I can't let this place be spoilt. I'll see to it."

The colour rose in her cheeks. He seemed to understand;
but she herself had no clear notion what there was to be understood. Besides, his last words inspired her with uneasiness.
What was he going to do? There was nothing, surely, that he
could do?

" I am afraid I've been rather silly," she said, and began

hastily to talk about other things; but that didn't prevent a dreadful thought from gradually taking shape in her mind. Wasn't her companion just the kind of man to act on a sudden impulse? Mightn't he go and buy all this land himself? To raise the money he might do anything! He had no common sense. It was appalling.

When she got up to say good-bye, her manner was cold and withdrawn. "I'm sure you are right not to worry about that signboard," she said. "And anyhow, I've been very tiresome, for obviously there's nothing to be done."

Without making any attempt to detain her, her host rose and followed her down the veranda steps; then he took the lead, and in exactly the same manner as before accompanied her back to her car. Before she got in they both glanced at the signboard with embarrassment.

"I hope you'll come again soon." He said this as if he really meant it.

She gave a smile.

"Do!" he insisted.

"Yes. But . . ." No further expression of her thoughts was possible. "Good-bye," she said hurriedly, and the car whisked her off.

As she was rolling smoothly along in the dusk her disquiet, far from diminishing, gained in intensity. "He must think me very odd, or, if he doesn't, the reason must be that he is very odd himself. How can he possibly guess what I feel? And even if he does guess, why does he pay any attention to it? It's not a thing to pay attention to. Besides, he doesn't know anything about me. He doesn't know who I am—or that I really mean ever to come back. At any rate, not in future years. And yet, if he buys the land, it will be largely on my account." She felt herself growing hot, she felt tears springing into her eyes.

A few minutes passed, then she took her courage in both hands. "What it comes to is this: I am going to buy that piece of ground myself. Now that I am so frightfully rich, there is no reason why I shouldn't. Having just come of age, too, I can do as I like. I shall buy it without telling Mamma. Of course it will be necessary to explain things to her afterwards —and even to Mr. Berkeley Pell, I suppose; and what I shall say Heaven only knows! But if I don't buy this land the hermit certainly will. Oh, my dear, idiotic man, what trouble you are getting me into! Besides, how am I to go about this

business? I shall have to do something quickly, or he will
step in before me."

Leaning back in the corner of the car, Paulina closed her eyes.
Her contemplated action was an outrageous violation of the
principles that her mother and everyone else had been instilling
into her with a special solemnity ever since her father's death
six months ago. She felt not only foolish but wicked. On her
return journey through New York Mr. Berkeley Pell would
hear what she had done. She dreaded that most of all.

IV

MR. BERKELEY PELL was great in such a very superior fashion
that comparatively few people had ever heard of him. When
Mr. Pringle, Paulina's New York lawyer, a very important man
in his way, first pronounced Mr. Berkeley Pell's name, he paused
a moment, then, as the light of intelligence did not appear in
either Paulina's or Mrs. Charlesworth's face, he proceeded to
illuminate them. He explained that while Morgans, Rocke-
fellers, Vanderbilts, and so on, had a greatness that was public,
Mr. Berkeley Pell's was a peculiar kind of greatness that hid
itself from the world. In the first place, Mr. Berkeley Pell's
money was four generations old, and, if he owned yachts, estates,
and race-horses, the world never heard about them; hardly
anyone, indeed, knew where they were. Even what he *did*
wasn't very generally known; never had he—nor any member
of his family for that matter—figured in a divorce case; and
although he was one of the most hard-working and public-
spirited men in the whole country, the newspapers never, never
printed his name.

Again Mr. Pringle paused, noticing with satisfaction that for
the first time in five interviews Paulina actually looked interested.
He paused so long, and looked so full of mystery, that at last
she asked point-blank what Mr. Berkeley Pell actually did do.
" Ah! " said Mr. Pringle, and then gradually unwrapped the
astonishing fact that what Mr. Berkeley Pell worked at night
and day was the giving away of his money. " Oh! " said
Paulina, disappointed. But Mr. Pringle looked at her gravely
and remarked in measured tones that to give away one's money
wisely, continuously, and well, was a task that called for the
very highest moral and intellectual qualities. Besides, he went
on, sometimes Mr. Berkeley Pell took on even heavier responsi-

bilities: sometimes, if approached with sufficient discretion, he would give advice. To the President, to a gathering of the world's greatest bankers, or even to a European State that found itself in difficulties, Mr. Berkeley Pell would on occasion speak a few quiet words.

Paulina opened her eyes wide and nodded in silence; whereupon Mr. Pringle went on to say that Mr. Berkeley Pell was a personal friend of his and that he thought he could arrange a meeting. Paulina joined her mother in suitable cries of gratification and thanks.

The interview took place a week later, the interval being filled with careful preparations. There were messages through Mr. Pringle, then letters were exchanged, then came a series of telephone conversations with private secretaries. These subordinates all had very urbane, reassuring accents. "Don't be nervous," they seemed to imply, "the great moment is approaching, but Mr. Berkeley Pell remains favourably inclined towards you. Keep up your courage, and all will be well."

So one morning at ten minutes to eleven (for even Mrs. Charlesworth had been anxious not to be late) they found themselves passing through the portals of one of New York's most impressive buildings. At the end of a long, glassy corridor they entered an express elevator which shot them up to the forty-seventh floor in half a minute. Another glassy, glossy corridor stretched before them, and presently they found themselves in a suite of quiet, empty rooms panelled for the most part in bleached oak, or Spanish walnut—rooms free of the vulgarity of ornament save for an occasional Old Master hanging unobtrusively here and there. In the quietest and remotest room of all sat Mr. Berkeley Pell, a small slight man of middle-age with grey hair, grey eyes, and a remarkably slow gentle voice. He came forward and held out the softest, silkiest hand that Paulina had ever touched; to both of them, but particularly to Paulina, his manner had a deferential stateliness by which he seemed to raise her to his own eminence without stepping down himself. The interview lasted not more than ten minutes, and for nine minutes he was merely making conversation; when, however, he did allude to Paulina's fortune, his voice took on a gravity and his face a high seriousness by which she was truly impressed. Somehow he made her feel that she, like him, belonged to the elect, and that it was her duty to realize it. Before she left the room the meaning of the words ' Money is power ' had for the first time penetrated her mind.

On their way out they were taken by Mr. Berkeley Pell through a room in which a Board Meeting was to be held, and he introduced them to several important personages. A very impressive atmosphere here reigned; for even when exchanging friendly banter, these great men were careful to flavour their easy familiarity with implications of high esteem. And as soon as Mr. Berkeley Pell had told them who she was, their politeness to her had the same quality. She was reminded of the handling given to a priceless piece of Ming by true connoisseurs. To her mother Mr. Berkeley Pell and his friends extended a courtesy that was perfect but with a difference. Paulina realized as she never had before that after all the money was not her mother's but hers. She found her consciousness of this rather embarrassing.

The next day was marked by another important event. Guided by Mr. Pringle she and her mother were taken to the home of the great Trust Company that guarded her securities. She realized vaguely that some ceremony was to take place, but the nature of it remained mysterious, for, if Mr. Pringle had disclosed it, he had done so in such terms that he might just as well not have spoken at all. After waiting in a quiet passage for a few minutes they were joined by a young man, who carried a large silver plate and a pair of large bright scissors. He invited them into a lift, which, instead of shooting up into the air, dropped them deep underground. After this there were a few stairs, a heavy door was unlocked, and the little party emerged into a long, long vault. Opposite was a row of shallow recesses, and these recesses were lined with safes which were let into the wall. The party moved slowly down the vault, the young man murmuring as they went. This recess contained the richness of Rockefeller, that the glory of Guggenheim, and in those two beyond there lay entombed almost half of the greatness of the Vanderbilts. Finally, after exchanging a knowing smile with Mr. Pringle, the young man halted before a recess not different in appearance from any of the rest. " Here, Miss Charlesworth," he said, " here we have the honour of keeping *your* bonds."

Paulina looked into the speaker's face, said, " Oh! " and giggled politely. The truth of the matter was that the hot, heavy air of the vault was making her feel more than a little sick. She had not (to use a frequent expression of her mother's) been taking an intelligent interest in the proceedings; nor did her guide's last words suffice to dispel her present non-compre-

hension. Although she had heard a great deal about bonds
during the last few months, she had never yet thought of them
as possessing a tangible substance; for her they belonged to the
realm of finance in which to the best of her belief there existed
only immaterial entities. She was now obliged to take in the
idea that bonds—although, like the blessed dead, they had their
true and essential being in an immaterial world—might nevertheless possess some sort of physical counterpart. She thought
of the catacombs in Rome, and the Tombs of the Kings at
Luxor (in both of which she had also felt rather sick), and with
a sudden flash of insight she grasped that bonds, too, were things
that could be reverentially housed in catacombs, tombs, crypts
or vaults such as this.

"I see!" she said with an expression of increasing intelligence.

But the young man, his head bent towards hers, continued to
regard her with an unchanging smile.

"I see," she repeated. "That's very interesting."

Satisfied, the young man drew himself up and let his smile
evaporate.

"And now," said Mr. Pringle, taking hold of her arm, "what
you have to do, my dear young lady, is to seat yourself here."

He made her sit at one of a series of tables that ran down the
entire length of the vault, and the scissors were put into her
hand. The young man, who had been complicatedly unlocking
a small steel door in the recess opposite, came forward with a
bunch of imposing envelopes. One by one, large, stiff, elabor-
ately-engraved sheets of paper were handed to her and from
each she had to cut off a strip. How curious it was! Each
strip, she was made to understand, might be likened to a rich
fruit that ripened with the passing of the months and years, and
must in due season be plucked. As she snipped them off, these
strips were placed upon the silver plate; and when all was
finished the party marched down the vault again and returned
to the upper air. Flushed and dazed, Paulina made even less
effort than usual to join in the conversation that Mr. Pringle
and her mother kept up all the way home. And they let her
be; it looked as if—for the second time—an impression had
been made. Was it too much to hope that she was at last
beginning to feel it her duty to fashion herself in the likeness of
Mr. Berkeley Pell?

V

THAT was a year ago; and in the meantime, although the influence of Mr. Berkeley Pell had diminished in spite of Mrs.
Charlesworth's persistent efforts to preserve it, the memory of
the great man was far from having completely disappeared.
So now, as poor Paulina leaned back in the corner of her car,
she was overwhelmed by the impiousness of the act she had in
mind; indeed, she could almost see upon the seat beside her
the cold, grey, dapper, little shade of Mr. Berkeley Pell, she could
almost feel the chill of his gaze and read his dreadful, unspoken
thoughts.   To part with bonds—bonds that were maturing their
rich fruits in the sultry, secret vaults of the great Trust Company
—to exchange them for a useless bit of Louisiana swamp-forest:
what could be more monstrous than that!   Hadn't he, indeed,
actually advised her to *sell* the real estate she already possessed?
—and that was proper real estate, not swamp-forest.

After a restless night Paulina rose early, her plans laid, her
resolution firm.   Briefly informing her mother that she was
going for a walk, she darted down the passage into the lift, and
a minute later had mingled with the busy crowd in the streets.
Two hours passed—two hours of concentrated effort; and then,
inwardly quaking but also inwardly triumphant, she was back
again.   The deed was done, the land was hers; she marvelled
at her own power.   And yet the courage to tell Mrs. Charlesworth how the morning had been spent was not in her.   No,
that was a matter to put off for as long as possible.   And in the
meantime to mitigate her sense of guilt she reflected that, if the
action was wicked, it had been performed, at any rate, in the
most irreproachable manner.   Not Mr. Berkeley Pell himself
could have been more cautious and calculating, nor could even
her mother have tried more painstakingly to drive a hard bargain.
The whole thing had been unspeakably unpleasant to her, and
that surely was to her credit.

Into her mind, engaged in these reflections, there crept all at
once a small, nightmarish doubt.   What if she had bought the
wrong piece of forest?   It wasn't at all easy to tell from maps
just where a particular bit of land lay or exactly what area it
covered.   Determined to do her job thoroughly, she had bought
quite a large tract; but supposing that she were to find that it
was the wrong one?   Abruptly she got up, slipped down to
the hall, and telephoned to the estate-agent.   She arranged
that he should accompany her to the site early in the afternoon

so that she should see with her own eyes that everything was all right.

. . . . .

"Well, thank God for that!" Deep was the sigh of relief, satisfaction, and triumph that Paulina breathed when, the inspection over, she found that she had made no mistake. Moreover, her boundaries were even more liberally inclusive than she had imagined. A really noble piece of forest was hers.

The agent duly thanked and got rid of, she looked up at the hateful signboard and gave it a grimace. " You ought to be lying on the ground," she said, " so that I could put one foot on you, like St. George."

But with all this elation she was also feeling agitated and uncertain. Although she had been near enough to his house to hear him chopping wood, she had not yet seen the hermit. Would he be offended at what she had done? Would his pride be up in arms? Had he, she wondered, been spending a disappointing morning in Pontchartrain, because some unknown purchaser had stepped in just ahead of him?

" I must feel my way and see how things go," she said to herself as she approached the clearing, and it was not without inward trepidation that she waved a hand to the man who was now engaged in stacking his chopped wood.

" How nice of you to come!" he cried. " I am being rewarded for my virtue, for I had a job to do and wanted to put it off to this afternoon, but then I thought: ' No, do it now!' So off I went this morning."

" What kind of job was it?' asked Paulina warily. " Worse than chopping wood?"

" Yes, much worse. I had to telephone."

She laughed. " Do you call that a job?"

" I do. Besides, the nearest telephone is a couple of miles away."

" I suppose it was something important?" said Paulina innocently.

He looked at her, grinning, and lit a cigarette. " Yes. I have bought this piece of land."

She stared, flushed, and then half turned away. " What do you mean? You can't have bought it."

" I have. I telephoned to my lawyer to buy it for me."

" But one can't buy land all in a second like that!" She frowned a little. " It can't be done—not like that."

" Why not?"

"Well!" She was at a loss. "What did your lawyer say?"

"He said he'd buy it right away."

"But has he?"

"I suppose so. Why not? I shall be very much annoyed with him if he hasn't."

"Perhaps he couldn't," Paulina said at last.

"Oh, I gave him a free hand. And this piece of land can't cost much."

Paulina began to feel bewildered. "Are you very rich, then?" she asked.

The man's face expressed considerable amusement. "Oh yes, I'm frightfully rich!" But the next moment seeing that she looked put out he quickly went on: "No! But this piece of ground can't cost more than ten or fifteen thousand dollars; and I have securities worth at least that much in the bank; and my lawyer has a Power of Attorney, and he's a hustler. So now we needn't worry any more."

"I don't quite understand," said Paulina, who was feeling too flustered to mince matters. "Do you mean that he'll sell some of your bonds?"

The man again looked amused. "Some of my securities— yes. I don't think I have any bonds."

Paulina was scandalized. "But don't you even know . . ."

"Oh yes, only I can't remember at the moment."

There was a silence; and Paulina's companion noticed that her face was taking on its most determined look. At last, a deep flush dyeing her cheeks, she took the plunge. "Please— won't that lawyer have to sell *nearly all* your securities?"

Staggered by such directness, her interlocutor hesitated, and his reply: "Oh dear, no!" came just a moment too late.

Paulina's eyes darkened with anger. "You are not . . ." she began, then stopped.

"Go ahead!" said the man. "You think I am lying."

"Yes."

"And being a fool."

"Yes," said Paulina again.

There was a pause. The man lit a fresh cigarette from the one that he had been smoking; Paulina, looking away, struggled with conflicting emotions. Here was someone with hardly a penny to his name, who went off and—behaved like this! And then he came back to chop wood and puff away at his cigarettes without a care in the world. It was abominable. It was indecent. Supposing Mr. Berkeley Pell had been listening to this conversation, what would he be thinking now? Paulina's imagination failed her.

The man was now putting on his coat. " I don't believe you've ever been to the bayou down there." He pointed towards the back of the house. " Let me show it you."

" Yes, please do! " Paulina's tone was one of extreme politeness. " A bayou is a canal, isn't it? "

" No, a bayou is just any waterway. But most of the bayous about here are artificial. They are made to drain the land."

Skirting round the house, he led the way down a narrow winding path under the trees. " Look at those ilexes! Aren't they fine? Have you noticed that my house is in a little oasis where the trees are quite free of moss? And down by the bayou again there is no moss. I am going to show you some of the best swamp-cypresses and sour gums that you have ever seen."

In the ten minutes' walk that followed Paulina's agitation subsided. Indeed her change of mood was so complete that she sank into an unusual peace. " He's a very odd man," she thought, " but I like him; and what's more I feel sure he likes me. As for the rest, it really doesn't matter."

When she came to the bayou she was overcome by its beauty. It was a straight, glassy avenue of water—nothing more than a very wide canal in fact—and yet it had a melancholy beauty that went straight to her heart. For a short distance on either side there were trees, then the trees fell away, showing a wide marsh, then there were trees again. A great solitariness hung over it. Suffused from above by the sky's faint coppery glow, it held the evening in its mirror, it held the evening of all evenings, the evening of life, the evening of the world. Its straightness carried you on and on—into depth after depth of contemplation. It was too sad to be anything but silent and still.

After standing motionless for a minute Paulina sank down upon a heap of dry rushes and continued to gaze and think. Then suddenly the impulse to speak came.

" I want to tell you," she began; and very incoherently she told him. Her name was Paulina Charlesworth, her mother was French, they had lived most of their lives in Paris. She had no memory of her father at all, for he and her mother had quarrelled and separated when she was still an infant. They had been rather poor until a year and a half ago, when by the death of her father she had suddenly become very rich. By the terms of his will she was obliged to spend at least one month

of every year in Pontchartrain.   Her father had belonged to an
old Pontchartrain family.   Charlesworth—the name perhaps
was not unfamiliar?

Here she stopped and looked up.   The expression she caught
upon her listener's face struck her as rather strange; but, when
he saw her looking up at him, he smiled; and never had his
smile been kinder.

She went on.   Soon she found herself describing Mr. Berkeley
Pell, and here they both laughed.   Then, taking her courage
in both hands, she gave an account of her morning.   " So—
so, you see, this land is mine."   As she said it the words sounded
very arrogant in her ears.   " I do hope you don't mind? "
Her eyes looked up at him timidly.

" Good Lord! " exclaimed the other in protestation, and
then made quite a long pause.   " I think you're a very nice
child," he said at last.

Paulina got up, gave a little laugh, and began to pick the
bits of dry rush from her dress.

Her companion helped her.   " It pleases me awfully to think
that all these trees are yours.   Surely this bayou is one of your
boundaries?   Can you remember? "

" Yes, it is," returned Paulina eagerly, and for the next half-
hour they discussed her boundaries with enthusiasm.

" You must come again to-morrow," said the man.   " You
must inspect every inch of your kingdom."

A cloud passed over Paulina's face.   " No. I'm sorry. I
shall have to put that off till next year."   And she explained
that she was starting back to Paris very soon, and that every
day until then was taken up with something.   " It seems dreadful to have to wait a whole year! " she concluded.   Her eyes
were again fixed on the bayou that was still glimmering in the
dusk.

VI

NEXT year, as her train steamed slowly into the station, Paulina's
eye fell upon a good-looking young man who was waiting on the
platform, and she gave a cry of astonishment.   It was Harry!
Not a word had Harry said to her in New York to prepare her
for his appearance in Pontchartrain.   He had evidently arranged
this as a surprise, he was reckoning upon her feeling flattered
and therefore pleased.   Well! it was really rather clever of him,

for she did feel pleased. Turning to her mother, who was
tipping the negro attendant, " *Voilà Harry!* " she said.

" *Mon Dieu!* " exclaimed Mrs. Charlesworth with emotion.
And Paulina heard her adding in a triumphant aside: " *Eh
bien! Ça y est.*"

During the long train journey Paulina's mind had turned more
than once to thoughts of the .hermit and the swamp-forest.
Her days in New York had been very crowded, full of small
excitements—to say nothing of Harry. It had been soothing
and restful to think about her new domain and the fun that she
and the hermit would have in exploring it. The unexpected
apearance of Harry altered this prospect completely; and an hour
or two later, after her first excitement had died down, faint
regrets flawed the surface of her satisfaction. One couldn't
step out of one mood into another at will or at the stroke of the
clock. " It means that I shall have to give up the idea of a quiet
time," she reflected. " I wanted to be by myself a little; I
wanted to stop and think."   And she glanced back over the past
twelve months, she went on: " I certainly have done a lot, and
most of it has been fun, but—well, I *was* looking forward to
something different—just for these few, weeks."

.   .   .   .   .   .

One can't have everything, however; and at teatime that same
day, seated at her dressing-table and surrounded by flowers
from Harry, she was listening with amused complacency to the
voices in the next room. It was Harry and her mother, who
never addressed one another without raising their voices; Mrs.
Charlesworth because she was talking English, a language in
which she was not at her ease, Harry because he was never
quite sure that Mrs. Charlesworth was understanding him.
Nevertheless, they got on very well together; and this, Paulina
reflected, was not merely because Harry happened to be a peer.
No, her mother would have liked him even as an impecunious
commoner (which, indeed, was just what he had been until
the recent death of his elder brother). Paulina didn't, as a rule,
like the people her mother liked; so it was fortunate that Harry
was an exception. In the first place, his appearance was satisfactory to them both. He had a small round head, reddish hair
cut very short, a ruddy freckled skin, and good features. He
was well-built, quite tall enough, and wore his clothes well.
His age, too, was suitable—he was thirty. Until recently he had
been in the Guards; now he looked after the estate, was active

in County affairs, and occasionally said something about agriculture in the House of Lords.

"I suppose this does settle it," said Paulina to herself. "I suppose I *shall* marry him. Why not?" She was in good spirits and feeling a little reckless. But that didn't prevent her from also feeling more than usually clear-headed. It was without hurry or carelessness that she now attended to her hair and the making up of her face, and when her mother's voice came to her through the door, "*Pauline, chérie!*" she smiled with amusement at its tone. "*Un instant, Maman!*" she called back gaily, nor was her own voice quite what it would have been had Harry not been there. Satisfied at last with her face and hair, she got up and turned in front of the wardrobe-glass. That reflection, too, was highly satisfactory, and she opened the door into the next room with happy composure.

Mrs. Charlesworth and Harry were sitting before a high, uncomfortable table which had just been wheeled in. The objects that bulked most largely upon it were jugs of iced water and mountainous napkins under which large squares of toast were wilting in their own steam. Mrs. Charlesworth continued to be busy with the teapot as her daughter came in, and for this Paulina was grateful. It was not many hours since she had last seen Harry, but she liked to renew her effect each time; and nothing cramped her style more than her mother's eye. Greatly did she now enjoy the look that came into Harry's face, his slight flush, his moment of speechlessness.

But her moods were apt to fluctuate most capriciously (a fact that she herself often deplored), and this little party, after beginning so well, became all at once distasteful. The mother, the suitor, the *jeune fille*—what a banal situation! Everything suddenly jarred upon her—her own smiles and gestures in particular. Falling silent, she left the conversation to her mother and Harry.

They chatted on; but she knew well enough that in a minute or two Mamma would tactfully withdraw, and then—no, Heaven preserve her! A proposal over this uncomfortable tea-table with someone waiting on the other side of a very thin door to learn the result—it was an intolerable prospect! She couldn't submit, she must make her escape.

Longingly she looked through the open window over darkening Pontchartrain and in a moment of nervousness began to tell Harry about the music from the pleasure-boat and the waves of emotion it had once aroused in her. She made it all sound rather amusing, but even as she was speaking, she disliked herself. To make fun of one's own feelings—it was very often just as bad as making fun of other people's. Of a sudden she broke off, turning to her mother with a little cry. " Oh darling! I've just remembered! There's something I simply must get before the shops shut. You and Harry go on talking; I shan't be long."

Mrs. Charlesworth was dismayed. " But, darling, the shops don't close for another hour."

" I know," said Paulina. " But I must fly."

" Well, but mayn't I come too ? " asked Harry.

No! She wouldn't have it. With great firmness she insisted that Harry must stay and talk to Mamma. Harry acquiesced.

In her bedroom, putting on her hat, she felt angry with herself, her mother, and Harry. She didn't want Harry to accompany her, it was true; but she was angry with him for acquiescing. Had he done it just in order to annoy? If that was the sort of man he was, she didn't want to marry him.

Hurrying out of the hotel, she walked aimlessly down the crowded street, and into her mind, which was searching for something less uncomfortable to rest on, there came again the thought of the hermit and the forest.

' I will go and see him *to-morrow*," she said to herself, " yes, I'll manage it somehow, and I'll tell him about Harry; perhaps I'll even ask for his advice."

.   .   .   .   .   .

But in spite of these resolutions there had to be a delay. Determined to keep her visit a secret not only from her mother but from Harry, she found no opportunity for the next ten days, and when at last she was able to set out her mood was one of considerable impatience. During the whole of this time, too, she had been feeling tense and irritable. Harry had proposed, and she had almost accepted him—almost, but not quite. She had kept a loophole; and, although sure she knew what was best for her, she wanted advice. But what reason had she to suppose that the hermit's advice would be of any use? She put this question to herself as she was driving out. What could he possibly know about people like Harry? What did he know about *her*, for that matter? His instincts were probably sound, but he knew nothing of the world—certainly nothing about the modern world in which she and Harry lived. Everything was so complicated; there were so many different sorts of considerations that had to be weighed one against another. The hermit was naïve and would simplify things too much. One could afford to be naïve if one lived by oneself in a swamp-forest; but she wasn't going to do that. And she sighed—almost wishing that she were.

The weather that afternoon happened to be dull; in fact, on stepping out of the car she felt a fine rain in her face. This was no day for the inspection of her property. Walking quickly down the track and through the wood, she soon had the familiar little house in front of her, and for a moment she halted, its squalid shabbiness acting almost like a physical check. The owner was to be seen as usual in the veranda. He was sharpening a hatchet and whistling as he worked; and the cheeriness (cheeriness, she said to herself, was exactly the right word) with which he greeted her was singularly out of harmony with the day—to say nothing of her own mood. When, smilingly, she reproved him for it he had no excuse—at least, not until it occurred to him to say: "It's seeing you again. Don't you call that a reason?"

"Ah, but you were whistling away before you ever caught sight of me."

The man laughed and stepped back to survey her. "How are you looking? I don't quite know." He laid a hand on her arm. "Have you been in Pontchartrain long?"

"About a week, and I had three weeks in New York."

"How is Mr. Berkeley Pell?" And he smiled.

"Do you know," replied Paulina, "Mother just didn't dare to tell him what I had done. Her courage failed her."

They went up the steps on to the veranda, and while her host was fetching tea, Paulina's mind wandered back for a moment to Mr. Berkeley Pell. A little sinister, a little pathetic, too, if you looked close; but, seen from outside, *comic*: that was how he now appeared.

"Well," said the man, coming back, "what have you been doing with yourself all this time?"

"A lot," said Paulina.

"Tell me about it."

"An account of the whole year?"

"Of course."

So Paulina got under way: Paris, the Riviera, Paris again, then London—a London season with Cowes and country-house visits afterwards. A yachting cruise, Aix, and then more Paris. Her recital was bare, but her answers to the hermit's occasional questions said a good deal. It was just as well, she thought, that the hermit should see that she was different from last year, that she had changed, become more grown-up—and perhaps a little cynical.

When she had finished a sudden gust of discouragement swept over her. To what purpose was she displaying herself in this light? Very likely she had done no more than raise a barrier between them. The problems of a sophisticated and disillusioned young woman were not within the hermit's competence. She looked at him speculatively. Just what he himself was, or had been, she couldn't guess at all.

After a moment she went on to tell him about Harry. She described Harry with a cool but not unkind detachment and felt that she was doing it well. " I shall probably marry him," she concluded, " and if I do I shall make him a good wife. Whoever I marry, I intend my marriage to be a success."

" How old are you? " her companion asked suddenly.

" Twenty-three."

" Twenty-three," he echoed, and while she lay back in her chair he surveyed her again. How pretty she was, to be sure!

" I daresay that seems young to you," said Paulina, " but I came out—more or less—at seventeen. That was in Paris in a very cosmopolitan society, and since getting this fortune—well, I've been about a great deal."

" Yes, but you're young all the same."

" In actual years, perhaps," assented Paulina quite readily. " But . . ."

" Time counts. I mean just the ticking of the clock, the passing of the days. Events, experience, can be speeded up a bit, but all the same . . ."

Fixing an alert gaze upon her host, Paulina prepared for brisk argument, but all at once discouragement again fell stiflingly upon her. The rain was now coming down in torrents, the warm dampness of the air made the powdering of her face almost useless; the wretched man opposite puffed at his eternal cigarettes without speaking a word. " His complete lack of any social sense is really rather trying," she said to herself. " Here I am! I have come out quite a long way in the rain to see him, and not one finger does he lift to make my visit a success. Besides, I have been confiding in him, and he makes no response. Isn't he going to say *anything*? "

A gay smile on her face, she leant forward. " Tell me," she said, " tell me all your thoughts! Are you thinking that

I'm not yet sufficiently grown-up to marry? Or do you disapprove of Harry in particular as a husband for me?"

To herself she was saying. " Of course, what he really disapproves of is my ability to take a cool, dispassionate view of Harry. I suspect him of being romantic in a rather old-fashioned manner. He would like me to be swept off my feet, to see no faults in my lover, and to marry 'for love alone.' Well, Heaven knows, I'm quite romantic at heart, only not exactly in that way."

She continued to smile gaily, and the other, smiling back, said all at once : " *My* marriage was a mistake. I married too young."

" Oh!" She was amused. " So you think I'm too young?"

" In a way."

" But——" She hesitated, seeking how to express herself nicely. " But our two cases don't resemble one another very much, do they?"

" I think they do. I was very like you at your age."

" Well!" thought Paulina, fairly staggered.

" Why was your marriage a failure?" she asked.

" Oh, incompatibility. We didn't really have very much in common."

" Who was your wife?"

" She was a manicurist."

Paulina again had to take a moment before replying. " But—as far as outward things go, Harry and I have a great deal in common."

Her companion smiled. " And so had we. But unfortunately a couple of years later she began to find that I was rather a drag on her and she divorced me. Very soon afterwards she married again, and *that* marriage has proved, I believe, a great success. Possibly you've met her—Lady Harpenden?"

" Well, I—no, really!" And Paulina gasped. " I stayed with her last autumn," she added.

" Is she still pretty?"

" Yes, very. But in rather a hard way, you know."

The man laughed, got up, stretched himself, and then stood looking down at her with an expression which she found slightly disconcerting.

" What a bore this rain is! I've been longing to go round your property with you," he said tentatively.

" Oh, it's much too wet to-day." And Paulina gave a glance

at her shoes. "Besides—well, anyway, to return to Harry, I understand that you advise me not to marry him."

"I don't somehow think it would turn out frightfully well."

"But, of course, you can't really tell."

"No, of course not." He sat down again, and pulled at his lower lip. "Well!—you might marry him and see."

"But surely—surely that's not a very sensible way to behave?"

"Well, one has to do something."

"Yes, but there is no great hurry. I mean . . ."

"You've been knocking about like this for five years."

Paulina made no reply.

"There's such a hell of a lot to learn in life," the other continued, his eyes fixed upon the misty tress. "One can't afford to waste time—ever."

Paulina gave a sigh, then suddenly became brisk and gay again. "Well, anyhow!" She was glancing at her wrist-watch. "I must be off! You haven't got an umbrella, have you?"

"Yes, rather!" He spoke with pride, but it took him some time to find it, and—Heavens, what an umbrella it was! However, it was better than nothing; and, as they walked sloshily up the track, Paulina took his arm. It had not been a very satisfactory meeting, he had not been very nice, and yet . . .

When they were within a few yards of the car she stopped. "Tell me," she said, looking away as she spoke, "shall I marry Harry? Shall I?"

Her companion paused, and she could not resist throwing an anxious glance up into his face. She shrank from receiving one of those casual, indifferent answers of his, and his expression seemed for a moment to indicate that one was coming. But all at once his face changed. "No, my dear," he said gently, confidentially. "Somehow I don't think I should."

VII

Four months later Paulina married Harry, and the event brought to an end a way of life and an orientation of thought that were becoming increasingly distasteful to her. Taken simply as an end to be achieved, marriage is less pleasing than in any of its other aspects.

Like most young women, she wanted not only to be in love, but to be in love with a man she could be proud of. Harry qualified fully in birth, physique and manners; as to intelligence, he was at any rate clever enough to remain a dark horse. She wrote to her friend: " I am marrying a man I can be proud of," and in the course of his reply he said: " Do you mean publicly or privately proud of?" Her momentary anger at this breach of good manners was wiped out by the thought that a little jealousy was after all no more than human. Harry was young, good-looking, and—and had every other advantage.

When next February came round, it was accordingly as Lady Bridgnorth that Paulina presented herself before the hermit; and this time all the circumstances of the meeting were perfect. The day was one of pale, mauve sunshine—the sunshine one gets in Louisiana after a touch of frost in the night. Upon the thin, tall, grey-bearded trees this wintry light fell strangely, making spectres of them—beautiful and rather absurd spectres, tattered, scarecrow spectres, who seemed to enjoy flaunting their graveyard gauntness in the full light of the sun. But beyond noticing that the air was full of a coloured brightness, Paulina had driven along the familiar road without giving thought to the outward scene. She was contemplating her own happiness, which was of a kind that seemed to match the day. It had amused her to dress herself with a particular care (combining extreme simplicity with great finish), although of course never had artistry run a poorer chance of receiving adequate appreciation. " However!" she thought, " if he doesn't look at one's clothes, he does, to do him justice, notice one's expression. And he will see that so far at any rate all is well."

They met on the scrubby little patch of ground in front of the house, its owner having run out in his shirt-sleeves to greet her. She had been hoping that he would look as pleased as he always had before; nor was she disappointed. And at once her pleasure leapt up to meet his. " How nice!" she cried. " I think you really *are* glad to see me—in spite of my being married." With that she flung up her arms and gave him a kiss.

But the meeting, just because it had gone off so well, set a high standard for the rest of the visit. Paulina, however, was feeling really gay; she kept up her chatter without difficulty; she made her host laugh a great deal. First of all they wandered about under the trees, then they wandered about over the house—a thing she had never done before. Inside, it was indescribably dingy. Not exactly dirty, but dingy with the dinginess of things outworn. And, remembering how she had betrayed her feelings at her first sight of the outside of the house,

Paulina smiled to herself. How clumsy she had been in those days!

After helping her host to make tea, she sat down with him in the veranda. "Look here!" he said presently, and produced a newspaper. She had already seen what he now showed her, but she gave an amused laugh. It was a large front-page picture of herself. "Daughter of William P. Charlesworth makes her first visit to Pontchartrain as Wife of Peer. Lady Bridgnorth says: 'I love Pontchartrain. I feel it to be my Home-Town.'"

"There's glory for you," her host remarked.

"Yes," said Paulina. "Isn't it fun!"

"And the things they say about you, very nice, too. 'Beautiful Young Wife . . . took London Society by storm . . . has entertained Royalty. . . . As popular in London as in Paris.' All true, I hope?"

"Every word!" laughed Paulina.

When the time came for her to go—and she explained that Harry had only given her a limited leave of absence—she felt that she had stayed long enough. Next time she came they would take things more quietly together.

"Please," she said, as they were walking down the track, "I want you to take me to the bayou next time. And let's go again just as the sun is setting behind those trees. Shall we?"

In reviewing her visit on the way back she was gradually overtaken by misgivings. One part of her talk in particular displeased her: a moment when she had been trying to give her host an idea of the actual shape and texture of her English life. She could see that she had conveyed the suggestion that she was a very *managing* person, one who was always pulling strings, and using her influence, and pre-arranging her effects. It was most unfortunate; because she wasn't—surely?—like that. But the hermit hadn't been at his best either. His touch, never light, had been particularly clumsy now and then. And at times he had also been rather facetious. Somehow or other, alas, she had made him feel constrained.

As she was passing the cemetery she looked out once again at the kennel-like tombs with the long shadows of the cypresses falling across them, and melancholy invaded her. Her companion had certainly been looking older, a good deal older. "Perhaps he *will* be in one of those soon," she said to herself, "and what shall I have done for him? And what will have been the meaning of our friendship? Shall I have reason to reproach myself? Shall I wish that something more had been said or done?"

The next day she sent a letter to her friend asking if she might bring Harry to see him, but an hour after she was sorry that she had done it. For one thing, it would cause her to look at him through Harry's eyes; and then it would also make her look at Harry through his eyes; and in all this there would be a kind of disloyalty. Not that either would be able to make her alter her opinion of the other, but she would feel impelled to explain each to the other. Already, in describing the hermit to Harry, she had fallen into the mistake of slightly romanticizing him and her relations with him. It was all a little uncomfortable.

A couple of days later she and Harry started out. That Harry had every intention of being nice was clear; but she was apprehensive that he might at moments become a little condescending in his niceness; and that, she felt, was certain to irritate her. As always, when her nerves were on edge, she was wearing her briskest manner, and her answers to everything that Harry said implied that his remarks were really not worth making. For instance, when he commented with surprise upon the tombs in the cemetery—"Well, obviously," she returned; "you can't bury people properly in water." Subjected to such treatment, it was only a matter of time before Harry got sulky, and sulky he soon became. She began to feel miserable. "Oh, you idiot!" she cried to herself. "Why must you choose to-day of all days to behave like that? Just when you wanted him to be in a specially good temper! There isn't time now to get him back into the right mood again. Besides, you aren't in the right mood yourself." Helpless and unhappy, she sat by Harry's side and Harry continued to look sulky.

But one never can tell. In spite of everything, the visit to the hermit went off exceedingly well. At first, it was true, Harry was rather unnecessarily polite, and the hermit a little jerky and stiff; but that did not last long. For her part she simply left things alone (for the very good reason that she was feeling unequal to doing anything else), and that policy turned out to be the right one. Moreover, Harry had been clever enough to be nice not only to the hermit but to *her*, and of course she had responded, so that the hermit had been able to see for himself how beautifully they got on together.

On the way back in the car she felt happy—pleased with the

hermit and Harry and herself. She thanked Harry for being so nice; and he replied: " Well, I think he's quite a good chap. Not nearly such an eccentric, darling, as you had made out. He's one of these nature-lovers, that's all. A regular type, you know."

" Don't you think," Paulina went on, " we might do something towards making his house a little less disreputable-looking? Really, the squalor is getting beyond a joke. That armchair of his is falling to pieces, the awning we sat under is full of holes. If we gave the house a coat of paint, which it badly needs, we could choose a less revolting colour."

Harry, to her great content, fell in with this idea. " Yes, why not! " he said. " I think it's quite a good scheme."

" Well, next time I see him I'll talk to him about it. It may not be easy to get him to agree, you know. But I'll manage somehow."

She managed without the smallest difficulty. As soon as she had convinced the man that his house really was shabby inside as well as out, he said: " Oh, very well, go ahead then! I expect I shall like it when it's done. It's very nice of you, anyhow."

So they proceeded to go over the house together, and this was quite amusing.

On getting back to the hotel, Paulina went up to Harry, and, full of her schemes, began telling him all about them. But, alas, it very soon became evident that the moment was not well chosen. Harry had come back from an unsuccessful after-noon's fishing to find among a lot of tiresome letters, two of a quite exceptional disagreeableness. One was from his brokers (he told her no more than that); the other was from their neighbour in England, Colonel Morgan-Williamson, who curtly refused to join the syndicate for the grouse-moor to which he had belonged for the last two years. This rebuff, Harry pointed out, was quite plainly the consequence of Paulina's behaviour to Mrs. Morgan-Williamson last year. " Damn it all! " he complained. " It isn't as if I hadn't warned you time after time that she was touchy and that it was particularly important to be nice to her." And he went on at considerable length.

Feeling depressed and unsuccessful (for the worst of it was that she really had tried to be polite to the wretched woman), Paulina went into her bedroom to read her own letters there. One was from her mother, a very characteristic letter, a letter that made Paulina frown, and smile, and sigh. Two were

begging letters; another was from a friend who was now in a
lunatic asylum. Suddenly all her vitality seemed to flow out
of her; sitting on the edge of her bed in the dusk, she felt—
not sad, no, that was too fine a word—she felt merely dreary.

She was still sitting there when the room suddenly became
filled with sound. It was the pleasure-boat's wailing call to
pleasure; and then, almost at the same moment, there came a
loud knock at the door. A messenger-boy entered and handed
her a telegram. Indifferently and abstractedly she opened it.
It was from a firm of Paris solicitors, who announced with an
exquisitely formal politeness that both her mother and her aunt
had just been killed in a motor accident.

The next day she and Harry started for Paris.

VIII

THE redecorating of the little house had accordingly to be
postponed (for its owner certainly wasn't to be trusted—and
indeed he definitely refused—to see to it himself), but next year
Paulina returned to the charge almost as soon as she arrived.
The outside and the inside of the building were both taken in
hand, and this gave her a reason—not that she really needed
one—for frequent visits, besides affording a ground upon which
she and the hermit could meet easily. During this month they
got on to more familiar terms than ever before, and although
there was no expression of intimacy, both felt that the seeds of
intimacy were there.

One afternoon, as they were sitting together under an ilex
outside the house, her companion's eyes rested upon her with
an expression which, had she seen it, would have caused her to
wonder. But she did not see it; she was mending a patchwork
quilt, a present for him, which she had found in Pontchartrain.
A checkered light fell through the branches of the great tree;
it was a very pleasant spot, which until quite recently had been
disfigured by empty beer-bottles and old tins. Paulina derived
great satisfaction from the transformations that she had effected.
A few minutes ago she had been pulling the furniture about in
the house with her own hands. Her hair was now untidy, her
light summer dress a good deal crumpled; and never, thought
the other, had he seen her looking more youthful or more
charming. At last, turning his eyes away, he gave a sigh and

said: "I find it difficult to think of you as a married woman. You don't give that impression."

"Well, really!" Paulina, without looking up, smiled. "Were you expecting me to look matronly?"

There was no reply.

"Now, listen!" said Paulina, threading her needle. "If, when I come back next year, I find everything squalid again, I shall be very angry. You treat your possessions so badly— even your books. You kick them about on the floor. Even *they* don't remain nice for long."

"Remain nice! You talk as if books were like young women, who exist only for the sake of appearances. The books I buy remain nice inside however much I kick them about. And as for young women, I might go on to say——"

"Yes, my dear, you might. But don't. We have agreed that generalizations about women——"

"I don't remember agreeing. I like generalizations on all subjects."

"That new book of yours on astronomy was already falling to pieces. I had to get it rebound in Pontchartrain."

"You would have done better to read it."

"I don't like astronomy. *Le silence de ces espaces infinis m'effraie.*"

"Ah, that shows that you have the usual mistaken way of looking at things. I read astronomy when I want to feel cosy."

Paulina was following her own thoughts. "You never met my mother, did you? She was a remarkable woman. She had no reverence at all for either the starry heavens above or the moral law within."

"Do you miss her?" asked the other, after a slight pause.

Paulina couldn't help giving a little laugh. "Yes. As a matter of fact I miss her more than I thought I would." She lifted her head to look dreamily into the trees. "We had a very dismal time in Paris, Harry and I. There were endless formalities; a host of completely-forgotten French relatives emerged out of their lairs and quarrelled over the will. Red tape, black crêpe, and pale, powdered, greedy faces, that's the picture it leaves in my mind. It made living and dying both seem rather sordid. I was glad to get back to Bridgnorth again."

"What did you do there?"

"Oh, lots of things—even a little reading. But not astronomy, I'm afraid. History, which you detest."

" And what did you think about?"

" I don't know. You, sometimes—quite often in fact."

" Would you like to have a child?"

Paulina put down needle and thread to light a cigarette. " Yes," she said at last.

" I suppose Harry would like a boy?"

" Probably." After a few moments she picked up a pattern-book. " Before I go we must choose curtains for your bedroom. Now, look here, you have got to have either this one or that. It's no use your looking at any of the others."

He took the book from her hand. " But surely *this* is very nice? I like the stripes."

" My dear man! Can't you see how hideous it is? Thank Heaven I didn't ask you to go ahead with this job yourself. I think you must have this. Yes." And she got up.

An hour later she was sitting at her writing-table in the hotel and Harry came into the room.

" Hullo, so you're back. How was the wild man of the woods to-day?"

" Oh, he's always the same. I hope you had better luck. Did you catch anything?"

" I haven't been fishing this afternoon." Harry sat himself down on the sofa and picked up a newspaper.

When Paulina next looked round it was to see that he was not reading but staring straight before him. She quickly turned and appeared to be busy with her letters, but in reality her mind was elsewhere. When Harry did this it always meant that something was up.

" I'm writing to say we shall be back in about three weeks," she said. " You don't want more than a week for our Washington visits, do you?"

" No. That's plenty." And Harry gave a loud yawn.

She felt sure that yawn was artificial, and deliberately she faced round to look. Yes, of course it was! Harry had the flushed face and the glittering eyes that certain kinds of thinking always produced in him.

" Ouf!" She pulled off her hat and flung it on to a side-table. " Isn't it terribly hot in here?" And her glance at the window was a suggestion that he should open it.

Harry ignored the hint; a gleam of amusement, as if he detected her nervousness, appeared—or so she thought—at the back of his eyes. " I didn't go fishing," he said. " I went to see Gulick instead."

" What did you want to see *him* for? "

" Well, I'm pretty sick of these Pontchartrain journeys, as you know. And I think that with Gulick's help we can fix things up all right."

She guessed what he meant, but she said: " Fix up what? "

" Oh, so that in the future we shan't have to come."

" *You've* never been obliged to come to Pontchartrain."

" I know that. Nor will you need to come now."

" I see. So that's what you are looking so triumphant about."

The word triumphant was justified by Harry's half-smile. She knew that half-smile of his only too well, and at this moment she disliked it quite particularly. Strange to think that in the old days it had attracted her. If it still spoke of something rather mysterious in his character, that something she no longer desired to understand. She thought: " Are we going to have a quarrel? And, if so, what about? "

Until quite recently she had agreed with Harry that a regular yearly journey to Pontchartrain threatened to become very tiresome, but now—now she felt differently about it. For one thing, it would give her—if Harry could only be persuaded to stay in England—a yearly holiday. There was no reason whatever why Harry should have come this year; he might have stayed in England and hunted, which was what he really wanted to do. But, although himself secretive and jealous of independence, where she was concerned Harry was both watchful and inquisitive. She had discovered very soon after their marriage that his off-hand, happy-go-lucky manners were in many respects misleading. For one thing, he never could trust anybody; and, although a singularly bad business man himself, he had probably come to Pontchartrain just as much to keep an eye on her business affairs as to look after her.

" I see you have a pattern-book there," said Harry. " The thing seems endless."

" No, no. It's all finished now. And anyhow, it was all on a minute scale, you know." She said this with a conciliatory smile, for there were times when Harry became irrationally and unaccountably stingy. It always made her uncomfortable when this side of him came to the fore.

To her intense relief he dropped the subject. What he did say was: " I think Gulick's quite a good chap, don't you? "

" Of course he is."

" He was rather odd in his manner once or twice this afternoon."

"How absurd you are, Harry! How was he odd?"

"He was odd when I happened to mention your hermit."

"Odd about *him*? What do you mean? And what made you speak about the hermit to Gulick?"

"Oh, I just said that you had gone off to see a man who lived by himself in a wood—a sort of Thoreau. I said it to explain why you hadn't come to the office with me."

Here Harry stopped; this was a trick of his, and to Paulina a particularly irritating one. It was necessary to say "Well?" before he would go on again.

"Well?" she said at last.

"Well, Gulick looked odd and asked if I meant the man who called himself Benson. I said I didn't know what he called himself."

"Benson—that *is* the name," said Paulina quietly. For some unaccountable reason she was beginning to feel a little frightened.

Harry sat looking at her for half a minute without speaking. Then, very deliberately, he lit a cigarette.

Paulina felt rather sick. "You might give me one," she said carelessly.

"Catch!" said Harry, and threw. "I rather gathered that Benson isn't his real name," he added.

"What is it then?"

"I don't know."

"Didn't you ask?"

"As a matter of fact I think I did. But Gulick passed on to something else. He didn't tell me."

"Dear me, how sinister!" said Paulina in a tone of impatience. And she laughed. But unfortunately sinister was just what she did feel it to be. Yes, Harry and Gulick, and indeed the whole world, had all at once become sinister. And she suddenly began to feel cold; her whole body felt chilled.

"Ouf! It really is getting *too* stuffy in here." Jumping up from her chair, she went and threw open the window. "I was stifling," she said as she suppressed a shiver.

"Gulick looked as if he might have told me quite a lot about that man," said Harry, who was watching her steadily with his fixed half-smile.

Paulina came and stood in front of him. For a minute she looked down through half-closed eyes. "All right," she said. "I suggest that you see Gulick again and find out all you can. And then, if there is anything bad, you can come and make the most of it to me. But I warn you, nothing that you say will make the slightest difference." And with that she went into her own room.

Harry laughed and picked up the newspaper.

IX

Two days went by during which Paulina and Harry were polite and a little more than polite to one another; in fact, they were carefully amiable. Then, in the afternoon of the third day, the moment that Paulina had been dreading arrived. She was lying on her bed, half-undressed and less than half-awake after her siesta, when Harry appeared in the room. His face was slightly flushed, his eyes bright. As his glance passed over her he smiled a little. "You're looking very charming," he said.

"I think you might take the trouble to knock. Will you please give me that dressing-gown?"

Harry continued to smile. "You look awfully nice as you are." And, leaning against the closed door, he continued to stare at her.

She got up, put on her dressing-gown, and stretched herself out on the bed again, her arms behind her head.

"Well! I've got something to tell you," said Harry.

"I knew that the moment you came in."

Harry's expression became slightly vindictive. "Your hermit has spent several years in gaol."

"Has he? Well, I expect it's much to his credit."

Harry gave a grin.

"Was he in gaol in this country?"

"Yes. In the State Penitentiary at Baton Rouge."

"Then without doubt it's to his credit," said Paulina.

At this Harry's grin developed into a chuckle. "My dear! Really! Wait till you hear!"

Paulina's heart contracted. "Go ahead."

Harry abruptly stopped laughing. "I'm sorry. But when I do tell you what it is, you will see that your last remark was really rather funny."

"I'm waiting," said Paulina with anger.

"Well, your hermit was gaoled for murder, but there were extenuating circumstances, so he got off quite lightly." Checked by a slight embarrassment, Harry paused a moment before adding: "The man's real name is Wentworth."

"Wentworth?—oh!" It took Paulina a few seconds to understand. Then, after a moment of faintness, she felt her colour coming back with a rush. "You mean, he's the man who killed Uncle George?"

Harry nodded.

"It's an odd coincidence, certainly," said Paulina evenly.

Harry looked at her with a certain respect. "You take it very well, I must say."

"Well you know the circumstances in which that killing took place. I think . . . Wentworth . . . was justified."

A scowl gathered over Harry's face. "I think you're taking it just a trifle too well," he said.

"I never knew Uncle George," returned Paulina coolly. "But judging from what I've heard about him he was a thorough scoundrel."

"Well, I'll be damned!" Roused to anger Harry came and stood over her by the bed. Paulina looked up at him with steady eyes; after a moment he moved away. Going over to the window, he turned his back on her.

"Has it occurred to you that, although *you* haven't known who *he* is, Wentworth has known very well who you are?"

Paulina winced; but Harry's back was still turned. "I think he has shown both good sense and tact. He let bygones be bygones. And now, having shot your little bolt, perhaps you'll go."

"My God!" said Harry in a voice of disgust. He gave her another look and walked slowly out of the room.

. . . .

It was a hot, damp night, an enervating night. After dining at a night-club and dancing, Paulina and Harry went home to bed early. Time passed, but they did little talking. Talking was what Paulina was determined to avoid.

After Harry had gone to his own room she got up, had a cold shower-bath and then read Byron's letters for an hour or so. The English Milord, so conscious of cynicism, so unconscious of vulgarity, did not help her much, and, looking at the thick, black volume which the hotel management provided, "I should have done better to read the Bible," she thought.

After putting out her light she lay staring up at the ceiling and trying to imagine *why*—just *why* the hermit had treated her like this. She also tried to recollect all that she had ever heard about her uncle's death. The case had been famous in its day. In the smoking-room of some club in or near the town an

Englishman called Wentworth had shot the Pontchartrain millionaire, George Charlesworth. In the course of the trial it had come out that Charlesworth had seduced Wentworth's second wife, a young Creole of great beauty, whom he had met and married in Havana only a few months before. There had been long accounts of the affair in the Pontchartrain newspapers which her mother had sent for. Paulina remembered that her father, William Charlesworth, had given evidence. For days her mother and Aunt Jeannette had talked of nothing else but this case.

How strange, how very, very strange, to think of the hermit as " that man Wentworth! " To think that he had this drama in his past! To think that he had spent years—how many years?—in prison. " And yet," she said to herself, " I am not really surprised."

A deep feeling of compassion invaded her, but she also felt deeply wounded. Why hadn't he told her everything? Wouldn't it have been quite easy? Didn't he understand her sufficiently after all these years to see that he *could* tell her? This concealment was not like him.

She dreaded the morning. Harry, she felt sure, would wake up in a bad temper; and the prospect of another talk with him before seeing Wentworth was intolerable. She thought of getting up very early and leaving a note to say that she had gone to the hairdresser. But she couldn't stay at the hairdresser's all the morning. And then there would be luncheon, and Harry couldn't be trusted not to embark on the topic even in the restaurant. And what of the next day? And the next? It was like that when one was married. No escape. Not until the greater part of the night had gone by did the thought flash into her mind: " But why shouldn't I go and visit the hermit *early*—just as early as I like? "

It was accordingly at about eight o'clock the next morning that she was walking down the familiar track. Familiar—and yet this time unfamiliar, for the freshness of the night was still in the air and the light came from the east instead of the west. It was a lovely, windless day; all the world seemed happy, and she couldn't help hoping that Wentworth, who was always quite cheerful enough, would not be actually " cheery." " If I find him whistling," she said to herself, " I shall burst into tears."

But he was not whistling. The house was silent, and to all appearances empty; not did her advance across the clearing bring the man running out to greet her. Slightly anxious, she mounted the veranda steps and looked in through the open door. Ah, there he was! She breathed a sigh of relief. He was sitting at a table writing, and so deeply was he engaged that not even now did he turn his head.

" You can put the things down there," he said, " and that's all, thank you. I shan't need anything else."

" It's me," said Paulina.

He started. " Paulina ! "

Bewilderment gave place to an expression of joyful surprise. " Oh, I am glad," he said.

" I hope you don't mind . . .? "

" Mind ! My dear ! " He sprang to his feet and seized both her hands. " My dear ! I might have known . . ."

She was silent. His manner puzzled her.

" I was trying to write you a letter." Slowly he gathered together the sheets of paper before him and slowly tore them up. " But I'm not good at writing. I am so glad you've come."

Together they went out on to the veranda, and he made a sign to her to sit down. She obeyed wonderingly. How on earth had he discovered that she had been told? It comforted her to find him deeply stirred, as he evidently was.

" *What* were you writing to me ? " she asked gently.

Wentworth frowned. " I'll tell you."

Sitting opposite he stared at her fixedly for a few moments, then went on: " I don't know how to say things—you must forgive me for being blunt. But the whole thing is so clear—indisputable. You and Harry must be divorced. There is no doubt about it. And that being the case, the sooner it's done the better."

" What are you talking about? " said Paulina.

Wentworth's frown deepened. " All these last weeks it's been in my mind. I've been thinking. And since yesterday I've felt quite sure."

" But I don't understand. What have you been thinking about? "

" About you and Harry."

" Since yesterday? " she stammered. " But I didn't say anything special yesterday. I haven't ever said anything to make you suppose . . ."

Wentworth made no reply, but he, too, was evidently puzzled; and his look was full of reproach.

" Perhaps," said Paulina, collecting herself, " perhaps I have given a misleading impression at some time or other. I'm sorry."

"No," said Wentworth. "You haven't given a misleading impression. That's just it."

"But I must have."

"No," said Wentworth.

"I swear to you——' began Paulina.

Wentworth rose and with so peremptory a gesture that she was silenced. "Listen, Paulina, whether you have meant to tell me as much as you have doesn't matter. The point is that I see the truth. There is no good in this marriage of yours. It is not good either for you or for Harry. It is holding you both back, and you mustn't go on with it. Have the courage to face the truth. There is no time to waste in life."

Paulina pressed her lips together; when she opened them it was to say: "My dear, I didn't come here in order to discuss my marriage. I have something else on my mind. Will you let me talk about it?"

Wentworth turned away. She saw that he was not only bewildered but in some strange way deeply hurt. With his face averted he said: "I suppose I have been tactless. I suppose I shouldn't have spoken at all. But, after all, during the six years that we've known each other I haven't said too much on the whole, have I?"

"No." Paulina gave a little laugh that was slightly hysterical. "Everything you've said in those six years could, I think, be put down on one sheet of foolscap. It's not too much."

There was silence. Then with a rush she went on: "Please! you mustn't worry about my marriage. It hasn't meant very much to me. That's all. And perhaps I am made like that."

"No, you are not like that."

"I wonder if you know," replied Paulina with a kind of bitterness. "Please listen! Not all people are meant for the same thing. My life is much more the kind of life I am meant for than you probably realize. Besides"—she paused—"if I have ever given you the impression that my life is empty I have deceived you. Perhaps I have unconsciously made appeals for sympathy. Women do. Perhaps I was romanticizing myself. The truth is that I find my husband and my home very agreeable. Indeed, why shouldn't I? I have everything that a young woman could reasonably wish for. Harry is very much in love with me. Bridgnorth is lovely; and I have plenty of friends— and plenty to do there. I have my job in life. I like to have a job and to do it. Although I sometimes grumble, as everybody does, I have a great deal more in life than most people, and I ought to be thankful."

Wentworth had listened to this with an expression of profound disappointment. At last he made a gesture. "All right," he said.

Why was it that at the sound of these two words Paulina was assailed by a deathly chill? But she summoned all her resources. "I didn't come here to talk about myself," she went on resolutely. "I wanted to ask you a question."

Wentworth was staring dully before him. "A question? What is it?"

"Why haven't you ever told me that you are the man who killed Uncle George?"

Wentworth looked round at her sharply. "Oh, you've heard that, have you?" He stroked his chin. "Well, after all, it doesn't make much difference, does it?"

She hesitated for a moment. "No. But—but why didn't you tell me?"

Wentworth sighed and then shrugged.

"Why didn't you tell me? Why?" She was trying to recapture some of her earlier feelings. "Don't you see that it was all wrong not to? Why did you leave me to find out through others? Isn't that the kind of thing that inspires mistrust?"

"Good God! Mistrust? Do you mean that?" He had taken a step towards her and his expression was one of dismay.

"No," said Paulina faintly. "I didn't mean it."

Wentworth flushed. "I suppose I am a fool," he said. "I took it for granted . . ."

"Yes," said Paulina quickly. "Yes, and you were right."

Wentworth was silent.

"But you are not always right," continued Paulina with resolution. "I swear you are not."

"For example?"

"Well, in being so—so very eccentric. You *can't* go about insisting on young women divorcing, when there is absolutely no reason why they should. You *can't* go about killing people's uncles, and then talking to them as if the matter was of absolutely no consequence. Please, please, my dear, don't go on like this! Don't turn into an eccentric! Don't, if only for my sake. Don't, because, then, what you say will lose all its weight with me. And I do need you and count on you."

To her relief Wentworth, thus adjured, looked neither angry

nor hurt. His eyes were resting on her calmly and speculatively, and at last he gave a smile. " Have you had any breakfast?" he asked.

" Yes. But I should like another cup of coffee."

" You shall have it."

He gave it to her. They talked for a few minutes more, but nothing of importance was said. And then they parted.

PART II

I

THE swamp-forest was wrapped in a low-lying mist above which the moon shone bright in a clear sky. Out of this sea of level mist tall tree-tops rose here and there. Some were like dark, weed-covered rocks uncovered by an ebbing tide, some—dead, leafless branches—were like the arms of drowning men. A few small owls flew about in the moonlight from one tree-top to another.

Underneath the blanket of mist Wentworth, standing outside his house, heard the owls calling to one another, and the sound moved him strangely, for it was this same cry that he had listened to, night after night, in his prison cell. In those days he had longed madly for the freedom to wander; and so now, when he woke to hear the owls calling, he would often get up, no matter what the hour might be, and go out under the trees. There was one spot that he was especially fond of visiting—a glade in a moss-hung and decaying part of the forest, where the trees were unusually large and grouped with a singular beauty. Sometimes by moonlight, but more often in the thick white darkness of the ground-mists, he would make his way to this glade and sit gazing down the broad avenue of ilexes whose forms loomed silvery and mountainous under their hoods of moss. Of the other trees in this region most had already been stifled to death, the moss hanging like rotten rags from their white skeleton bones.

On this particular night, as Wentworth stood outside his house in the dark, thoughts of Paulina were in his mind, for she had sent him a telegram to say that she was about to sail for New York, and that he might expect to see her in about a month's time. Two years had gone by since their last meeting, and he knew nothing of how she had fared in the interval. " I should like her to see my glade by night," he now said to himself. " Some time or other I think I must take her there."

For the next half-hour he was feeling his way along under the trees, streamers of moss brushing against him as he went, festoons and canopies of moss looming into visibility overhead, and the moon a faint, pale disc immensely far away. Arriving at the glade, he sat down and waited for the dawn. The owls had now stopped calling to one another; there was a hush, broken only by a faint, distant wail—the hoot of the American railway engine that has a note of melancholy mixed with menace. And that brought Wentworth's thoughts once more back to Paulina.

. . . . .

About a month later at this same hour, Paulina woke to the sound of a similar hoot, but louder and more menacing, for it came from the engine of her own train. The luminous dial of her travelling-clock told her that in another two hours she would be in Pontchartrain. Putting out her hand she raised her window-blind, and without lifting her head from the pillow looked out at the misty night-shrouded landscape. As light increased she began to recognize parts of the country that had attracted her attention before. There was a long bridge over the arm of a lake; and now as always a blue, misty opalescence lay on the surface of the water. On the other side of the lake the train halted at a small station in an ilex grove. Behind the station house there was a green grass-plot planted with palms, magnolias, and banana-trees, the dark foliage of the ilexes making the background. This was the frontier of the country that she associated with Wentworth.

From the rack beside her she picked up his last letter and read it over again. The writer said he was "awfully glad" she was coming; he hoped she was well, and that this time she would "make a good long stay." Still holding the note fast in her hand, Paulina lay back on the pillow and remained for a long time staring straight in front of her. "*Shall* I make a good long stay?" she wondered. "Perhaps I shall. Perhaps —who knows?—I shall stay there for good and all."

"But will the hermit want me?" she went on. "Will he like me as much as he used to now that I am so maimed, so defeated?"

She continued to ponder. "I have always wanted to come to this place alone; but first it was Mamma who accompanied me, and then it was Harry. Now at last I *am* alone—quite alone."

Shutting her eyes, she turned over on her side and tried to go to sleep again. But her thoughts were not under control, and before long tears were trickling from beneath her closed lids. "I have failed in everything," she kept repeating to herself. "Through my own folly, I am left with nothing at all." She thought of the last look Harry had given her in court; he was unable to feel forgiving even in the moment of her defeat.

In a little while she got up, and, as she sat at the window, looking at the familiar marshlands, the thought of Wentworth was a comfort to her. " It won't be necessary for me to say much, nor will he talk much. I shall be able to sit in complete silence for as long as I please. I shall be able to loiter about in the swamp-forest for as long as I please. That is what I need."

It was in the afternoon of the same day that she found herself again walking down the well-remembered track. "Eight years!" she murmured to herself. "It is actually eight years since I first came stumbling along over these ruts, staring at the palmettos which were new to me and sniffing at the strange swamp smell. The air is warmer than I have ever known it before. But this time it is already spring. I should like to know this place, as the hermit does, in all the different seasons."

Slowly, with frequent pauses, she wandered on through the trees, and the thought came to her that she was feeling more nearly what she had felt eight years ago than at any other time in between. In the interval she had experienced moments of intense recollection but never quite *this*.

When she came to the edge of Wentworth's clearing she stood still and gazed; she wished that he were in the veranda, she wished he would come hurrying down the steps to greet her. And then something unexpected happened. Out of the door of his room there stepped—not Wentworth, but a young man whom she had never seen before. With the air of one who is in his own home, the stranger lit a cigarette, threw himself down in a chair, and opened a book. A wave of terror swept over Paulina; a voice within her said: "You have come too late. The hermit is dead. The place has passed into other hands. Now you are indeed alone." For a minute or two she was without the power of movement or thought; then, urged by her very fear, she went forward.

The young man raised his head. Staring hard, he rose to his feet, but, even after she had reached the foot of the veranda-steps, he continued to do nothing but stare.

Controlling her voice with a great effort, " Does Mr. Benson no longer live here?" she asked.

The young man looked as if he hadn't heard; then, suddenly flushing, he replied: " Oh yes, he's here all right."

Her relief on hearing these words deprived Paulina of speech, and to hide her emotion she turned her head away. All at once

Wentworth's voice sounded from indoors. "Who's that? That's not Paulina, is it?"

Paulina wanted to answer, but couldn't. She glanced at the young man appealingly; but he, although his eyes were still fixed on her, seemed once again to be lost in abstraction.

"Is that Paulina?" Wentworth called out again.

"I think," the young man stammered, "I think it is."

"Splendid!" cried Wentworth. "That's splendid! Stephen, you ass, show her in! Why don't you show her in?"

Paulina ran quickly up the steps and into the room. Wentworth was lying in bed, and in such a position that she cried out at once: "Oh, my dear, have you broken your leg?" She hurried up and kissed him on the forehead. "I *am* sorry! Is it a bad break? Tell me quick."

Wentworth's eyes were bright with pleasure. "How are you, my child? Damn it all, you don't look too well, do you? Turn to the light so that I can see."

"No," said Paulina. "I think I would rather not. Tell me about your leg."

"Oh, as for that—it was a simple fracture. Another few days and I shall be hobbling about."

Something—perhaps it was the presence of the young man in the veranda—made them both feel self-conscious.

"I wonder," said Paulina, glancing round, "how do you manage here all by yourself? Is there no one to look after you?"

"A woman has been coming in during the day; and as for the nights, Stephen——" The latter's appearance in the doorway caused him to break off. "You're not going away yet?" he said.

Stephen stood there rather awkwardly, a suit-case in his hand. "Yes, I'm already late."

"Good-bye then. Shall I see you to-morrow?"

"Yes, sometime to-morrow. Good-bye." And Stephen disappeared.

"That," said Wentworth, "is a very nice fellow. It was lucky for me that he happened to be here when I broke my leg. Ever since then he has been sleeping in this house. Uncommonly good of him, considering that he has to be in Pontchartrain at half-past nine every morning to give a lecture."

"Shall you be alone to-night? I think you ought to have somebody with you."

Wentworth dismissed this with a headshake. "Tell me

something about yourself. That black dress doesn't mean mourning, does it?"

Paulina gave a faint smile. " No, I am not in mourning."

She was sitting by the bed now with her hands in her lap; and there was something in the quietness of her pose and expression that made the other look at her long and thoughtfully. " Two years! " he said. " It is two whole years since you were last here."

" Yes." Paulina drew herself up with a little decisive movement that he remembered well. " Yes, and a great deal has happened. I think I had better tell you now, if I may?—and get it over."

" Please! "

She knit her brows and looked away. " You know I had the intention of making the best of things. Well, soon, somehow or other,~everything went wrong. I don't know what happened, but I suddenly found I wasn't doing anything with my life. I wasn't even getting satisfaction from doing my duty and having the kind of success I aimed at. Perhaps I wasn't so very successful after all. I wasn't, in spite of my efforts, providing Harry with the kind of wife he wanted. Gradually I hardened myself and became defiant. I had a love-affair. And that was quite exciting for a short time; but I wasn't very much in love. I think I am rather like a man in not attaching much importance to the physical side of things—when there is nothing but that. My lover knew I wasn't really in love with him, and when I gave him up, although he was rather unhappy, he was not at all surprised. Then I had another lover—and it was the same thing over again." She paused. " How dreary it all is to look back on! "

There was a silence until Wentworth said: " What about Harry? "

Paulina bit her lip. " Harry and I were getting more and more estranged. He didn't yet suspect me of having lovers; but he saw—just as I saw—that we had different views on everything, on life as a whole. I had discovered that Harry is very conventional, that he cares very much about ' keeping up his position ' in London, in the County, everywhere. He clings to the old social order and to his privileges, and I never realized how little I was in sympathy with that attitude to things until I came up against it in him. And even then, if he had been able to feel a little more detached, we might have found a common ground. But it was not enough for him that I was willing

to play his game; he insisted upon my thinking it a very fine
game. At first I was rather impressed with everything, you
know. I was proud of Bridgnorth Hall and the rest of it. But
really"—her eyes filled with an angry light—" one has to be a
fool to make that the centre of one's life. A fool!"

"Oh well!" said Wentworth, and then added: "I dare say
if you had really *loved* Harry . . ."

Paulina was silent, looking at him fixedly.

After a moment, "Go on, my dear;" he said, gently.

With a sigh she collected herself. "After a year I became
quite reckless. I behaved without any regard for my reputation
or for Harry's name. And all at once there was a scandal.
Then Harry turned upon me; he had every right to turn upon
me. He started proceedings, and I was foolish enough to fight
the case. It was not a nice case, and he made it worse than it
need have been."

Paulina turned her face away. "I don't think I shall ever go
back to England again."

Wentworth put out his hand. Paulina took it and held it.

"Well, anyhow, that's all over now," he said.

"All over," echoed Paulina.

II

As she drove back to Pontchartrain that evening Paulina said
to herself that she would certainly return after dinner and spend
the night in Wentworth's house. "And not that night only,"
she thought, "but every night until he is well enough to move
about a little. I don't think he'll mind."

Accordingly, a few hours later, she was once again making
her way up the rough track. The light of her electric torch
guided her, for there was no moon, and the night was still and
dark. At the edge of the clearing she paused. A glimmer of
lamp-light from Wentworth's window seemed to show that he
was not yet asleep. "But we won't talk any more to-night,"
she said to herself. "He looked tired, and we have plenty of
time before us. How happy I am to be here. In that house I
shall find a kind of peace."

She went forward again, moving very quietly; but before
going up the steps she announced her presence by saying in her
ordinary voice: "Are you awake? It's me. It's Paulina."

There was no reply, and after waiting a moment she went up into the veranda. Looking in through the open door, she saw Wentworth lying asleep, the lamp beside his bed, and an open book in his hand. She went in, and as she stood by the bed, a feeling of tenderness and protectiveness swept over her. "His face would make a fine death-mask," she thought, and it surprised her that she had never seen before what she saw now. When Wentworth was awake his face was marred by a look of strain or pain, but sleep uncovered a profound peace.

Seating herself by the bed, she sank deep into meditation, and so remained until roused at last by fatigue and the chill of the damp forest air. She got up, extinguished the lamp, and by the light of her torch went down the veranda to the other room. A few minutes later she was in bed, nor was it long before sleep overtook her.

.   .   .   .   .

Footsteps outside suddenly brought her back to a consciousness of her surroundings. Her eyes fastened upon a beam of light that came in through her open door. She was not frightened, for the next moment she heard Wentworth saying, "Hullo, Stephen! What are you doing here?"

"Sorry to wake you, but I found Pontchartrain unendurably hot and noisy. So I decided to come back. You don't mind?"

"Of course not," was the reply. "Except that you came back for quite another reason. Wait a minute, and I'll light the lamp."

Paulina, lying still in the dark, smiled to herself. "Poor Stephen! What will he say when he comes into *this* room?"

The smell of cigarette-smoke now drifted in to her. A syphon was used, ice clinked in a glass. Of the talk that had begun not very much reached her, or rather, as soon as she heard that they were discussing the Great Slump, she became inattentive. Stephen was evidently bringing back dramatic tales of fresh disaster and panic; banks were closing, ruin spreading, there was no knowing what the end would be. Although nearly half her fortune had disappeared already, Paulina was unable to feel any great concern. Even her pity for others was, she realized, half-hearted. Then for a few moments the conversation turned on to herself. "Who is she?" asked Stephen. Wentworth's reply was inaudible and brief. "Oh, I see," said Stephen and paused. "I think I read something about it in the papers." There was a silence, after which Wentworth went on to talk about the book that he had been reading, a book about the stars.

Not long after this she heard Stephen get up and she could tell that he was stretching himself and yawning. " Well, I won't argue with you to-night, Tom. I'm going to bed." His footsteps came to the door. " A lovely clear night!" he said. " By the way, I have just had another letter from Dibdin. He tells me he has spotted a new nova. ' Another White Dwarf gone west,' is his comment. Silly ass! How does he know? To-morrow he'll be equally confident about some other theory. These astrophysicians and their cosmogonies make me tired. If you want real science you should read my paper on *Diamagnetism in Thallium Single Crystals*."

Wentworth laughed and said something that Paulina couldn't catch; but the next moment he raised his voice to call out: " Take my lamp along; I don't need it. And shut the door, will you? The night's getting cold."

Paulina heard the sound of the shutting door, and at the same time a glow of lamp-light fell upon the wall of her room. " Five steps along the veranda and he will be here," she thought; whereupon, raising herself upon one elbow, she waited.

Stephen, a lamp in one hand and a suit-case in the other, walked in, stopped, and gave a noticeable start. She said in a low voice: " I'm afraid this is dreadfully tiresome for you. Will you shut the door and then I'll explain. It would be a pity to rouse Tom again, wouldn't it?"

Another moment passed, then Stephen put down the suit-case and shut the door. The lamp he kept in his hand, and while he stood there in the middle of the room looking at her, she took stock of him. He was clean-shaven and fair-haired, and there was a certain wildness in his blue eyes, which were, however, very deeply set. The light from the lamp showed off the modelling of his chin and mouth, which were both beautifully formed. His slightly hollow cheeks and long, thin nose gave him an ascetic aspect. Tall, large-boned, and spare, his figure and face both had an angularity that well accorded with his slightly Scottish accent. " He looks fanatical," thought Paulina. " A hard, shy, arrogant young scientist, that's what he is. I suppose he is about thirty-five. He must be nice, if the hermit likes him."

" I am very sorry," she said again, " but, as you see, here I am. I didn't like the idea of Tom's being left quite alone, so, without saying anything to him, I came back after having dined at my hotel. The same thought must have occurred to you. And the question now is . . ."

For a considerable time Stephen answered with nothing more than a stare; at last, however, he said: " I can go back. It's quite simple."

" Oh, but that would be such a pity."

Stephen said nothing; and again the fixity of his gaze struck her as rather odd. She waited.

" I don't mind going back." Stephen pronounced these words absently; moreover, he showed no disposition to act upon them.

" I think that would be a pity," Paulina said again. " And Tom would be disappointed at not finding you here in the morning. I could hardly dare to face him."

" Oh, I don't know," said Stephen in the same dreamy way.

A disconcerting idea was taking shape in Paulina's head. " Is this *le coup de foudre*? " she sardonically wondered. " If so, nothing could well be more inconvenient. But no! " She measured Stephen with her eye. " He doesn't look that type."

Stephen now moved slowly to the chest of drawers and put the lamp down. " I could, I suppose, sleep in the veranda," he said.

" Yes." There was a little uncertainty in her voice now. " Do do that, if it won't be too uncomfortable."

" There are two mattresses on that bed," said Stephen. " Do you think you could spare one of them? "

" Of course," said Paulina, and, after a very brief moment of hesitation, she got up.

Stephen came to the bed and jerked the lower mattress from underneath the other. While he was taking it to the veranda she slipped quickly in between the sheets again. He returned, went to a cupboard from which he drew out some blankets, and then paused by the door. " Good-night," he said shyly.

" Good-night," said Paulina.

.   .   .   .   .

When she woke the next morning the sun was shining in at the window. It was six o'clock. Happy to be where she was, she lay still and smiled. But her pleasure in being in Wentworth's house was slightly marred by her memory of Stephen. She had wanted to be quite alone with Wentworth. It had never entered her head that her swamp-forest might be invaded.

When she was dressed she opened her door and looked out. The veranda was empty, even the bedding had gone, nor was

Stephen anywhere to be seen. With a sigh of relief she went out into the sunlight and at once took the path down to the bayou. "Will it be as lovely in the early morning as it was in the evening?" she wondered. "Is it really as lovely as I remember it? Shall I be disappointed?"

She was not. When she came out on to the bank, she stood entranced—just as before. There *was* something specially beautiful about this scene. The straightness of the bayou made it unlike any river; it seemed rather a path for angels, its glassiness reminding her of the glassy sea in the old hymn. Filled with peace she wandered a little way and then sat down on a cypress log. A few hundred yards further on a man stood looking down into the water. He was a fisherman, she imagined, and she thought no more about him until he began to move in her direction, and then she saw that it was Stephen. He was walking very slowly with his eyes fixed upon the ground; but she presently realized that he must have seen her, for when he was quite near he lifted his head, said very quietly "Good-morning," and then sat himself down on the other end of the log. She was pleased to find him in a mood attuned to hers; it would have been intolerable had he begun making conversation. While he sat there with his eyes fixed upon the bayou, he trespassed so little upon her sense of solitude that she became oblivious of his presence. It was not until some ten minutes had elapsed that she began to feel a change. She was now turning her back on him, and gradually there crept over her the sense that his eyes were fixed upon her. No longer was she able to lose herself in contemplation of the scene. For several minutes she resisted the impulse to turn, but at last had to yield and threw an unwilling glance over her shoulder.

Her eyes met Stephen's, and he said: "I want you to dine with me to-night. Will you?"

Paulina turned away again. If she had not resented his joining her, it was because his presence at first had been no intrusion. But now all her peaceful thoughts were put to flight. Stephen's words dragged her back into a world where there was no serenity, a world of which she was weary. A brief refusal was on her lips when she remembered that he was a friend of Wentworth's; and to this there was added a sudden conviction that he was very much in earnest. "Besides," she said to herself, "he is at least being direct, and I owe it to him to be equally direct. I must make him understand as quickly as possible that he must leave me alone. If I dine with him I shall be able to explain things. I don't want him to feel uncomfortable when we meet afterwards."

She turned again and looked at Stephen full. "There's no particular reason why I shouldn't dine with you to-night, if you really wish it. I was intending to go to Pontchartrain this evening to pick up my letters and collect some more clothes. But you won't find me a very lively companion, I'm afraid. I am tired. I have come here for the sake of solitude—much as one might go into a retreat."

She once more looked pensively down the bayou. Stephen drew a deep breath. "Thank you for saying yes," he replied and rose to his feet. "Will it suit you to be at Celestin's at eight?" Paulina nodded. And on that he walked quickly away.

III

IT was a warm still evening. The broad street, gay with coloured lights, was filled by an excited crowd. Although seven had only just struck Stephen was already on his way to Celestin's. He walked quickly, with a look of profound preoccupation on his face. As he was turning into the narrow street that led to the old French Quarter, a pale, drunken man stepped across his path.

"Say, you!" and he took hold of Stephen by the shoulder, "I ain't got a cent left—not a God-darned cent. Funny, ain't it? Like hell it is."

"Quite," said Stephen.

"You blasted Englishman," said the man, "for two cents, I'd——"

"I know," said Stephen. "And if you want a dollar for a drink . . .?"

"Keep your muck," said the man. "An automatic—that's what I want."

"Sorry; I haven't got one." And, freeing himself with a jerk, Stephen went on.

Outside Celestin's he looked at his wrist-watch. "Nearly an hour to wait. Perhaps more. She'll be late, I suppose." Entering he sat down and ordered a cocktail. The plain, pale, bare room with its floor of little hexagonal white tiles, its simple, cane-seated chairs and general unpretentiousness, was very familiar to him. It was a good place to be dining at, for here one could sit and talk. Very soon he was trying to imagine what Paulina would look like when she came in, and he called up the various pictures of her that he had in his mind. First of all, there was the pretty, slender, fair girl in the thin black dress that he had seen coming towards him in the clearing. Her particular slenderness, her particular colouring, the particular intelligent childishness of her blue eyes—they had stirred something deep within him from that first moment. For him those eyes had such an appeal that he could never think about them without being overcome by tenderness. Nevertheless, as he now reflected, she was very far from giving an impression of insipidity. Even in those first minutes when she was so anxious, so terrified—for she had evidently thought that some harm had come to Tom—even then something of her true character had been apparent.

Then next there arose an image of Paulina in bed. He remembered the curve of her breasts under that very pretty, very thin night-gown, and her hair brushed back for the night, and the rather excited look in her eyes—a look that belied her air of coolness and self-possession. And then there was Paulina sitting on the log by the bayou. He had been thinking of her so hard before she came that her actual appearance had almost been an interruption. He had been thinking that it was difficult to associate the Paulina that he knew with Lady Bridgnorth of newspaper fame. How would she be looking when presently she came in? More dressed up, more like Lady Bridgnorth, he supposed. "What is to come of this?" he asked himself with a sudden angry frown. "What good *can* come of it? And, on the other hand, if nothing comes of it, that will be hell."

When, a few minutes later, she did appear fresh misgivings assailed him. All his hours of thought about this young woman did nothing to alter the fact that she was a stranger; perhaps they had nothing in common; how could he tell?

She accepted the cocktail that he offered her. "Yes, please. I do need one dreadfully. I admit that I'm very tired."

Paulina said this with an air that completely belied her words. And yet her words were true, and she wanted Stephen to believe them. The day had not passed at all as she had expected. To begin with, after lingering by the bayou long enough to make sure that Stephen must have started for Pontchartrain, she had gone back eager for breakfast and for a long, comfortable talk with Wentworth, in the course of which she would find out something about Stephen, so as to be prepared for the evening's encounter. But the moment she had got to the house Wentworth had waved a newspaper before her eyes and questioned her regarding the state of her affairs. " Oh, anyhow I shall have plenty to live on," had been the gist of her reply, but this had not prevented him from insisting that she should go straight to Pontchartrain to see what could be done. " A 'bus passes in ten minutes' time," he said; and her protests had been sternly disregarded.

Her sitting-room at the hotel, just as he had predicted, was full of telegrams and telephone messages. All day, accordingly, obedient to his exhortations, she had hurried from one business appointment to another, but always with the sense that her time might be better spent. However, she didn't really care. At five o'clock she lay down on her bed with a bad headache, and in the course of the next two hours she was several times on the point of sending a message to Stephen to cancel her engagement. At seven, after looking at herself in the glass, she again wavered, then suddenly sprang into action. She telephoned for a hairdresser; in the meantime she had a bath; at eight the transformation was complete.

At the door of the hotel she met one of the University professors whom she knew, and from him she was able to learn something about Stephen. The young man specialized in crystallography and was accounted a genius in his own line, having already made one or two discoveries of the first importance. After a journey to Russia three years ago to inspect the famous new laboratories at Kharkov, he had come back to London to announce that he was converted to Communism and had accepted a high position in Kharkov University. For the last two years he had lived in Russia, engaged in research work, and he was returning to Russia at the end of his present tour—in fact, he was sailing from San Francisco in a week's time.

" Is he married? " asked Paulina.

" Yes. He married a Russian girl several years ago. He has left her in Kharkov. They have a child, I believe."

" Well," said Paulina to herself, " I really don't see any reason why I shouldn't try to enjoy my evening. Stephen, I'm sure, can be quite impersonal if he chooses. His Communism, his passion for science—these fit in perfectly well with my conception of him. There is something hard and decisive in his make-up which I like."

Looking across the table, she now said: " I met Professor

Berry just now, and he has told me all about you. You are a Communist and a crystallographer, whatever that may be, and you live in Russia. Do tell me something about it."

Presently they were discussing Stalin, and from that they went on to the quality of hardness in character, and its habitual association with wickedness. Paulina said that she admired hardness, and Stephen thought: " There is Lady Bridgnorth speaking! " And he felt chilled. But the conversation flowed on, and the excitement of being in Paulina's company did not diminish. Indeed, it was much heightened when after a while he became aware that she, too, was excited. As the minutes went by they grew more and more interested and lost their self-consciousness. Soon they were springing from topic to topic like two prospectors who have discovered a new, rich goldfield, and are hurrying breathlessly from one find to another before settling down in earnest to dig out the ore.

When they next looked round the room it was to observe with surprise that the other diners had all disappeared. Paulina glanced at her watch.

" You can't go yet," said Stephen.

" Oh yes, I must. Besides, this place is closing."

" We will go somewhere else, then, where we can dance and have supper."

After a moment's hesitation Paulina acquiesced.

In the taxi she was saying to herself: " He knows who I am, and I have told him I am unhappy. I have even told him why. He knows I am in the mood to snatch at anything that will give me a few minutes of forgetfulness. After that warning he must look after himself."

A little later they were dancing, and they danced for quite a long time. When they came back to their places Paulina's face was slightly flushed and Stephen's eyes again had an intent and yet absent look. Their talk now was desultory, consisting of little brief comments on what was going on around them. " I attract him," Paulina was thinking, " but I don't want only that. I want his friendship as well." The question was: Did he want hers? She was conscious of his holding a part of himself back. She was afraid he mistrusted her.

After a while they were dancing again, and during this dance, without looking up, she said: " I am enjoying myself." Stephen made no answer, but she knew that he had heard; and when they were back at their table he began making love to her.

"My dear Stephen," she presently interrupted, "how often have you said these things before?"

"Never before—at least, not like this. This time——"

"Oh yes," she smiled. "I know. 'This time it is different.'"

Stephen smiled too, but inwardly he felt desperate. "Listen!" he said. "You know very little about me. Perhaps I, too, am miserable. Perhaps I, too, am suffering from a sense of defeat. Will you let me tell you about it?"

"Yes," said Paulina slowly. "Yes, that is what I should like."

But instead of beginning Stephen knit his brows, and on his face she saw a look of indecision. Half-humorously, half-appealingly, glancing up at him, she said: "You know, I really am not otherwise than 'nice.' Can't you believe it?"

Stephen gave a short laugh. "If you are *that* as well as everything else . . ."

She waited. But there was silence again, until suddenly Stephen pushed the table away. "Don't you find the heat and the noise in here almost too much?" he exclaimed. "Is there nowhere else we can go?"

"Yes, to my hotel, if you like," said Paulina.

.   .   .   .   .

The night was hot and airless. It seemed very hot to Stephen, even up here on the sixteenth floor with the wide view down to the river. While Paulina was in her bedroom, taking off her cloak, he stared down over the roofs to where the distant pleasure-boat threw a confused blur of coloured lights upon the water. Out there, he reflected, people were dancing, drinking, and making love—and doing so all the more furiously for being filled with anxiety or despair. "How we are all caught!" he said to himself, suddenly aware of the rapid beating of his own heart. Then his thoughts went out to the little house in the forest. The beautiful, remote calm of death was a devastating criticism upon the petty, complicated, frustrated act of living. And yet Tom, who was now living right under the shadow of death, still rendered to life a simple and eager allegiance.

When Paulina came in he went quickly across the room, took her in his arms and kissed her. She yielded, but for a few moments only.

"Stephen, look!" she said. "I have put on my motoring-coat. You must forgive me for being so changeable, but I feel I must go back to Tom."

After a pause Stephen said: "Perhaps," and together they left the room.

He drove her out to Wentworth's house himself, and he drove fast, not because he wanted to, but from the tension of his nerves. A silence had fallen upon them, and it continued as they walked up the track. The night was clear, but the moon which was still low gave very little light.

When they came to the clearing Paulina looked up into the sky. "Do the stars really not interest you?" she said.

"Interest me? Of course they do."

"Last night——" she paused—"last night I overheard part of your conversation with Tom. You seemed to imply that astronomy bored you."

"No, that was just an old joke between us. I always accuse him of being mystically-minded—which he certainly is; but all the same . . ."

"What?"

"Well, I have no real objection to mysticism of his particular brand."

Paulina paused, then said: "Will you tell me about that— as well as about yourself—some other time?"

"Yes, if you will let me."

Treading softly they went up the steps, and Stephen took Paulina's suit-case into her room. When he came out he put his hands on to her shoulders and looked deep into her eyes. "Good-night." And after kissing her gently, he went away.

IV

"Go on," said Wentworth; "having begun, you can't possibly break off." They were sitting together at breakfast, and Paulina had been momentarily interrupted by the entrance of the mulatto maid. "Go on," he repeated. "After that excellent opening I am expecting great things. So you and he dined together?"

Paulina was looking very pretty. It filled him with pleasure to see in her eyes the light and sparkle of life. At this moment she was wearing "her wicked look"—a look that charmed him.

"Well!" said Paulina, and then stopped. She was feeling rather nervous, although her tone was light. "Well, we had dinner together at Celestin's—and I liked him. He's nice."

"He is. I like him, too."

"And he likes me. In fact, after dinner, he told me he loved me." Her eyes were dancing, but her breathing was noticeably fast. "Does Stephen always love everybody at first sight? Is it a habit?"

"No. I don't think so." Wentworth paused. "In fact, I'm sure it's not."

"Dear me!" said Paulina, and she got up, ostensibly to carry out the breakfast-tray, but really to hide a look of pleasure which she felt incapable of dissembling. She had woken up happy to be where she was—in this house, with the prospect of long quiet times with Wentworth. She was determined to make him feel that she could add something to his life.

On her return, she said: "I want you to talk to me about Stephen. He doesn't talk easily about himself, does he? But fortunately I met Professor Berry in the hall of the hotel and he supplied me with the main facts."

"What did he tell you?"

"Oh, about Stephen's becoming a Communist and his living in Russia, and his marriage and all that."

Wentworth looked at her thoughtfully. "What more do you want to know?"

"A great many things. But just as Stephen himself was ready to become more communicative, we discovered that it was very late—time for me to come back. Tell me! how seriously am I to take him?"

Wentworth frowned, then smiled. "Stephen generally means what he says."

Paulina hesitated. "Tom, I didn't come here for this sort of thing, you know."

"I imagine not."

"But—he interests me. Last night he made me forget for the time being how unhappy I was."

"Are you in love with him?"

"No. But he attracts me. I admit it—to you. When he makes love to me I like it."

"Are you going to dine with him again to-night?"

"Well—I want your advice about that."

"I don't know enough."

"About him?"

"About you."

Paulina hesitated again. "I think I know what you mean. Well; there was a moment last night when I might have done anything. I was reckless, and he attracted me and made me forget. Tell me, what shall I do? You are so wise."

Wentworth laughed. "Wise! Good Heavens! Look at my life!"

Paulina smiled. "How can I, when I know practically nothing about it?"

"I assure you, I have done all the stupid things there are to do."

"Tell me about them. All I know about you is that you were once married to the present Lady Harpenden."

"Well, that was a pretty stupid position to get into, wasn't it? Then I married Rosita, and that didn't turn out very well, as you know. I have also made three fortunes—by luck; and lost them—through stupidity. There you have my whole history in a nutshell."

"Oh, you are unfair to yourself."

"And that also is stupid. Let's go back to Stephen."

"Very well," said Paulina, smiling; and then with a change of tone she went on: "Tom, shall I dine with Stephen to-night? Shall I? After all, I see no reason why I shouldn't. I am my own mistress now." She laughed a little bitterly. "I see no reason why I shouldn't be his—for one week. Am I being foolish or wicked?"

After a brief pause Wentworth said: "I should dine with him, and get him to talk about himself."

Paulina opened her eyes wide. "Has he anything dreadful to tell?"

"Oh no!"

"He said he was disillusioned and felt defeated," said Paulina. There was another silence.

"You see," said Paulina, "I think he has really fallen in love with me—as seriously as one can in so short a time; and he is going away in a week. Is there any harm in my doing what he wants instead of sending him away with a sense of frustration?"

"I don't know."

"No," said Paulina with a sigh. "Of course not. How can you know? It all depends . . ."

"He is giving a lecture this afternoon at six," said Wentworth suddenly. "I think it might interest you to go to it."

For a moment Paulina looked surprised; then she said: "Yes, I see. That's a good idea. I should like to see him at his job."

"After that, go and dine with him, and get him to talk."

The lecture-room was crowded, and Paulina felt certain that Stephen had not caught sight of her. He spoke in a clear, rather harsh voice, but not in the manner of one delivering a lecture. At times he walked up and down the platform so deeply plunged in thought that some of his listeners looked at one another and smiled, for he gave the impression he had quite forgotten his audience. The lecture was an advanced one; hardly a single sentence was comprehensible to Paulina, but, as she mockingly confessed to herself, she was none the less interested and impressed for that.

At the end of the lecture questions were asked, some of which, coming from experts, were evidently not easy to answer. Stephen would then take time—plenty of time—to think out his reply; and it was in these intervals of his intense concentration that Paulina found herself most drawn towards him. He was sitting in a chair facing his audience; and while he gazed—lips compressed and brows furrowed—over their heads, she could not but hold her breath; and if the reply was long in coming, the strain became almost unendurable.

When all was over she remained in her place, waiting for his eye to fall upon her. He did see her at last, and his face as he came forward was smiling; but the smile rested upon a surface of deep preoccupation, and she remained aware during the whole of their walk to Celestin's that he was only giving her half his mind. "All the same," she said to herself, "I believe that since last night he has been thinking about me a good deal."

She was right. So obsessed had Stephen been that he had hardly slept at all. At last, however, the very intensity of his exaltation had forced him to come back to earth. "What is the use of being a scientist," he asked, "if one cannot examine oneself with coolness? This is the moment for a little detachment, to say nothing of common sense. What are my intentions? All my life up till now I have had a purpose—I have had my work. Am I, for the sake of this woman, prepared to abandon my purpose? Where is my passion for Paulina going to lead me?" He asked himself these questions, but they didn't interest him. How to win Paulina was the only problem his mind would attend to. "At this stage," he reflected, "in spite of our friendship, as lovers Paulina and I are pitted against one another. Love is a contest, the man playing to win the woman, and the woman playing not to be won, or to be won only at her own price—the price, very often, of a love more deep and enduring than the man is at first prepared to give. And in that the woman is justified. But," he went on, "if the man sometimes *merely* desires the woman, the woman sometimes desires *merely* the desire of the man. Vanity is apt to enter in on both sides; in fact there is very little love, in its beginning at least, that is free of egoistic taint. So the man and the woman are not only in conflict with one another, but each is the battle-ground of internal conflicts as well."

Part of the morning Stephen had been obliged to devote to the preparation of his lecture, and he was dismayed to find what an effort this cost him. "To be in love," he reflected, "is a form of insanity. And yet my whole desire now is to bring Paulina into a condition similar to mine! The heart in its passion knows neither reason nor pity. I am possessed, and nothing will satisfy me but that Paulina should be possessed too. What happiness can either of us possibly find in this madness?—Yet a woman," he went on, "is always waiting and wanting to love. And although with one side of her nature she wishes that her love shall be a voluntary surrender and follow where admiration and trust have prepared the way; yet she also needs to feel it as a force external, compulsive, dæmonic. A woman cannot really give herself; she must be given. And so the man must address himself as much to the dæmon as to her." With these thoughts Stephen had felt sadness creeping over him; he wished that love could spring out of tenderness and friendship alone.

. . . .

On reaching Celestin's they sat down at the same table as before, and at once the mood of the previous evening caught him up, everything else being forgotten in the pleasure that Paulina's presence gave him. His eyes wandered over her and he smiled.

"First of all," she said, "I want you to talk to me about Tom. I have the impression that you know him much better than I do. Although I am very fond of him I don't really understand him. What did you mean last night when you said that he was a mystic?"

Stephen leant back and half-closed his eyes. "I can tell you more easily what I did not mean. I did not mean that Tom was a nature-worshipper, or a dreamer, or a quietist. No, there is very little nonsense of that kind about him. Nor is he lazy. In fact I know no one with a livelier intellectual curiosity. But his mind is undisciplined, untrained. An incorrigible intellectual tramp—that's what he is."

Paulina laughed. "That's what makes him so fond of astronomy. I suppose journeys to the stars are the longest and most exciting of all."

"Exactly. I often complain that his interest in science is more romantic than scientific. I, as a hard-boiled scientist, believe in discovering the truth, not inventing it. Tom retorts that science moves by the imagination, that logic itself rests upon intuition, and that facts are interesting only for the light they throw on the whole. His subjectivism seems to me to rest on scepticism; I call him cynical. He replies that my objectivism is cynical in another way—besides being at bottom naïve."

" Oh! " said Paulina.

Stephen smiled. " Am I becoming incomprehensible? Ask me some definite questions. That will be better."

" Well, what does Tom *do*? Why does he live such an isolated life? It is not as if his prison experience had embittered him. But is he happy? "

" I think he is happy—in the sense of having come to terms with himself and the world. He lives alone because he dislikes society. By society I don't mean human beings individually, I mean social atmospheres. Up to the time of his imprisonment he led a very active life. He was a successful mining prospector and engineer."

" I know. He made two fortunes and lost them."

" Lost them! He gave them away. Not very wisely perhaps, but only too well. And now, having reached the age of sixty, he believes that the best he can do—not merely for himself but for the world—is to obey his nature, follow his thoughts. He believes that the ideal of self-illumination and the ideal of social duty are not incompatible, and that at his age what you think, and what you are, become more important than ' good works.' I feel this to be true—at any rate in his case."

" When you say that he dislikes society——"

" I mean he disapproves of it. And I have always found myself in agreement with him. It seems to me that in society the sense of the brotherhood of men is almost completely lost. Society encourages the spirit of competitiveness and the cult of appearances—and it is these that make men callous and cruel, trivial-minded and self-deceiving. It is the ideal of Communism to establish a community in which each individual is *primus inter pares* instead of a society in which rivalry and public opinion make slaves of all. That is why I became a Communist."

" Are you still a Communist? "

" In principle, yes—although Russia has taught me that in practice I can't manage it. When I went to Russia I was full of enthusiasm." He gave a short laugh. " I wanted

" to fan
And winnow from the coming steps of time
All chaff of custom, wipe away all slime
Left by men-slugs and human serpentry."

I was young and foolish, but I also genuinely wanted, like Keats, ' a fellowship with essence.' It is my fault that in Russia I haven't found it."

Stephen spoke these last words with great sadness. There was a silence in which Paulina lifted her eyes to him, but he was looking away.

" I suppose," she said tentatively, " I suppose you have talked to Tom about this? What does *he* think?"

" Tom finds excuses for me which I can't honestly accept. I know I am quite unpardonably influenced by the ugliness of life over there, by the absence of all graciousness and grace. I can't stand the crudity of thought or the bad manners."

" I don't think *I* should like Russia at all!" Paulina exclaimed with warmth.

" Perhaps not." Stephen leant back to survey her with a smile. " And yet if you had had my convictions, I fancy you would have stuck it better than I have."

Again they were silent.

" As for our Western society," Stephen went on with a change of tone, " let us give the devil his due. Competitiveness, snobbishness, vanity and pride have done more for civilization than all the virtues put together. It is they that have lifted men out of savagery. It is as cabotins, snobs, bullies and bluffers that we find the energy to hold ourselves erect and live with style. The panache, the fine gesture, how tempting in themselves! and what prestige and applause they always command! For centuries we have toiled uphill under these incentives, but now, I truly believe, unless there comes a spiritual change, we shall be carried over a precipice. Tom is more in sympathy with Russia than with the rest of Europe, although he utterly rejects any form of atheistic religion. I mean any deification of the state or the community."

Paulina sat very still, looking down at the table. " What does your wife think about all this?" she asked suddenly. " Is *she* a Communist at heart?"

" My wife? Oh, she doesn't bother about these things at all." And Stephen smiled.

" What is she interested in?"

" Well, chiefly her own beauty."

Paulina looked up. " Is she very beautiful then?"

" Yes, very."

There was a pause. Both felt that they had come to the point where generalities must be abandoned; yet both remained hesitant.

At last Stephen said: "When one comes to think of it, Caroline's absorption in her own beauty is less extraordinary than my absorption in the structure of crystals. We all of us . . ." He left the sentence unfinished.

"Caroline?" said Paulina nervously. "That's an odd name for a Russian, isn't it? Or did you re-christen her?"

Stephen looked puzzled. "But Caroline isn't a Russian. Good heavens, no!" He gazed at Paulina with growing astonishment. "Surely you know who my wife is?"

"I was told by Professor Berry that you had married a Russian. Who is your wife then?"

"Well!" Stephen paused, he was now looking embarrassed. "Tom is by way of being my father-in-law. Didn't you know that?"

Paulina stared, her face changed, she summoned a smile. "Did you marry a daughter of the present Lady Harpenden, then?"

"No. I married Rosita's daughter."

"What? The daughter of . . ."

"Yes, the daughter of Tom's second wife—the Creole."

"Heavens!" For a moment Paulina could say no more; and then they both began to laugh. "Tell me about your wife," said Paulina presently. "You say she is very beautiful?"

"Very," said Stephen. "She has so much beauty that she has never thought of anything else all her life. She is one of those women who are completely preoccupied by their beauty—obsessed. Not for a single moment is she unmindful of it. Poor child, it is hardly her fault. She is never in the presence of a man or a woman who lets her forget it."

"Even in Russia?"

"Oh yes! Even in Russia."

Paulina looked down and was silent for a few moments. "What did you mean by saying that you were 'by way of' being Tom's son-in-law?"

Stephen hesitated: he had a smile, but a strange one. "Well, there was that affair with your uncle, you know."

"Ah!" In a flash she understood. "So your wife is my uncle's daughter—and my first cousin! Oh, Stephen, how amusing!" And again she summoned a laugh, which to Stephen sounded natural enough. "What a charming surprise!"

Stephen laughed too, but with a note of uncertainty.

"Oh, but this is too amusing," Paulina went on, talking with great vivacity. "You must tell me more about Caroline,

Stephen. And about Matthew. I have the right to ask questions now, as a relation. Don't forget that." She put her elbows on the table, and settled herself as one prepared to listen. "First of all, tell me what Caroline looks like. Describe her."

And Stephen was made to talk.

V

IT was dark and still under the trees. Paulina was sitting in Wentworth's favourite place—on the log where she had seen him for the first time eight years ago. Between the leafy branches overhead the stars here and there were visible. Not the faintest whisper of wind sounded among the dry leaves at her feet; the night everywhere about her was dark, empty, and silent.

With a bitter pride she contemplated the firmness with which she had insisted upon Stephen's bringing her straight back from Celestin's, and took what pleasure she could from this self-inflicted pain. At Celestin's, outwardly composed, inwardly tormented, she had persevered in making Stephen talk to her about Caroline and Matthew; then, after he had driven her home, she had bidden him good-night in the veranda as before; and now here she was—alone.

Leaning forward with her chin in her hand, she sat quiet, and, as the minutes went by, the silence of the forest became more and more dreadful to her. Its silence was the voice of her loneliness. She was surrounded by it, she was engulfed; she felt it freezing her heart. "This is my lot," she thought. "And it will be like this to the day of my death." Tom, Stephen, Caroline and Matthew belonged together; into that group she had no right to intrude. Nor was there any other place where she belonged. To these thoughts the inhuman silence of the forest said: "Yes, it is so."

When she lifted her head it was to see a faint light shining through the trees. At this she shrank back, for the thought came to her: "If he has woken up, I ought to go and see if he is in need of anything." After a minute she rose, but the next moment sank down again. "I will wait a little longer," she said to herself. "Perhaps his light will go out."

But it did not go out, and after she had sat looking at it for a while, she felt compelled to get up. On her way back to the house, she composed her features and tried to compose her mind. As soon as she set foot on the veranda steps she heard Wentworth calling to her.

"Yes, it's Paulina," she answered gaily, and went in and stood by the bed. "Tom, why aren't you asleep?"

"I was afraid you were getting cold out there," he said.

"Oh no! It's quite warm to-night."

Wentworth was holding up his hand and appeared to be examining the lines on his palm. "You were a long time out there."

"You heard me go out then?"

"Yes, I heard you."

She did not know what to say, for she knew that her pretences were vain.

"I wish you would stay and talk to me a little," said Wentworth. "I don't seem able to sleep."

"Of course I'll stay. But I'm feeling very stupid to-night. So *you* must do the talking." And drawing up a chair, she sat with her back to the light.

"I liked to think that you were sitting on my log. I could tell which way you were going by the light of your torch through the trees. I have been thinking about you. When I lit my lamp it was a signal to you to come back. I thought you had been out there long enough. I mean long enough to get the feel of the night."

"The feel of the night—oh yes, I got that."

"I am afraid you may have felt lonely. But you were less alone than you thought, for here was I thinking about you."

Paulina smiled. "Dear Tom, you are very comforting. But——" she paused—"don't *you* sometimes feel rather lonely?"

"Not here. I live here, not in order to be alone, but to feel connected. It so happens that in this place I feel particularly aware of the intertwining of our spiritual roots. That feeling comes up, I think, from the earth. We all have our feet upon a common earth, our bodies are all built up out of a common mould, we all spring from similar ancestors, we all share similar memories through them:—it is in the feel of the earth that we get the feel of humanity."

Paulina looked at him speculatively. "I wonder what it was that drew me to this spot eight years ago? What is the attraction of this part of the world for us both?" She laughed. "Do you think we were here in a previous incarnation?"

Wentworth smiled. "Not long ago all this region lay under

the waters of the Gulf. It is unlittered by the vestiges of human history; and that is one of the things that attracts me to it."

"But you said that here you felt specially connected."

Wentworth was silent for a moment; then he said briefly: "Yes. But I want to feel the essential and not the particular, the archetypal and not the historic. Tell me," he went on in a different voice, "what has Stephen been saying to you? Whatever he has said, I feel sure you needn't be unhappy about it."

Paulina made a sound that was half a laugh, half a sob. "First of all, he told me who he is married to; and that came as a shock to me, because Professor Berry had said something quite different. *He* said that Stephen was married to a Russian woman. What must you have thought of me this morning when I talked glibly about becoming Stephen's mistress! As a matter of fact, I said what I said very largely in order to persuade myself, in order to convince myself—in order to get over another feeling."

"What feeling?"

Paulina looked away. "I don't know. Yes, I do know. It was——" Again she broke off, then said with a kind of anger, "I felt that to give in to him would mean too much—to me. To him, too, perhaps. Or it might mean too little to him. In any case, I felt it would be dangerous. Yes, I had already felt that."

"I see," said Wentworth.

There was a silence; then, with her eyes turned away, Paulina said: "Tell me something about the child—about Matthew. Stephen says he is remarkable."

"There is a photograph of him in that desk over there—a snapshot lying loose somewhere among my papers. See if you can find it."

Paulina made no reply; but after a moment she got up and went to the desk. While she was turning over the papers Wentworth went on: "As you will see from the photograph he is very nice-looking, very healthy and strong. But he is also unusual. He appears to have inherited his father's special gifts. In some respects he is almost a prodigy. And I daresay Stephen has already told you that he is getting an education that no child has ever had before. It is an interesting experiment. Matthew," and Wentworth laughed, "will be deep in Minkowski, Riemann and Einstein before he has ever learned the multiplication table or heard of Euclid."

While he was speaking Paulina had brought the photograph

to the lamp. She was bending over it, and Wentworth saw tears gather in her eyes.

"Did Stephen say anything to you about Caroline?" he asked suddenly. "I mean, did he describe his family life at all?"

"Not much," said Paulina faintly.

She was now sitting down again beside the bed. "Talk to me about something else," she went on. "About yourself. It will do me good."

"Very well. I will try to explain why I am not lonely here. I am convinced that in addition to contact through individual relationships, there is contact through the earth. And awareness of this is a comfort. All our ancestors down to the first speck of jelly from which we derive had a home somewhere on this earth, and their memories are somehow condensed and stored up in each one of us. In the womb you have gone through every phase of your ancestral life in swift recapitulation, and your ancestral life is alive now in your instincts and intuitions, your comforts and discomforts, in the whole tone and trend of your unconscious and conscious being. In my own case, sea-memories are particularly strong. I become very aware at times that for thousands and thousands of years my ancestors lived in the sea, or rather on that bit of seashore that is uncovered at low tide." He paused, and thoughtfully lit a cigarette. "If, when we die," he went on, "we mix temporarily in a crowd of spirits, some of which come from planets belonging to other suns, we of this earth will be easily recognizable, I believe, as earth-creatures. All spirits must, I am sure, be deeply stamped with the mark of the planet from which they come, and it is to his own planet that each will gravitate spiritually in any re-birth that may come to him."

"Even if he hasn't been particularly happy there?" said Paulina.

"Yes. That will make no difference. The fundamental ties are much too strong. You know how one feels about one's past even in this brief present life. When a whiff of real animal memory floats across the mind, how astonishingly poignant the emotion is! The actual substance of the memory is generally slight enough—hardly more than a gossamer thread. And yet the emotion is overpowering—and tantalizing in a unique way. Moreover, it makes very little difference whether the moment remembered was a pleasant or an unpleasant one. Now think —just think of the thousands, the millions, of years of accumulated memories that lie at the base of one's consciousness and bind one to the earth! Think what a tremendous force of feeling is there stored! I conceive of that force as the equivalent in the spiritual world to what gravitation is in the world of matter. It holds us earth-creatures together to form an earth-spirit as compact and distinct and unique as the globe of the material earth. The ordinary man's feeling for Nature is a dim, dim apprehension of this.

"There are certain nights in this forest," he went on, "when my sense of contact is quite extraordinarily strong—warm misty nights when the heavens are shut out and everything is still and near and intimate. And then there is quite another sort of experience that comes to me at times. It comes on nights like this, nights without either wind or mist or moon, nights when the stars are out. My spirit seems to project itself into the heavens so that the earth appears beneath me as a small solitary globe, and I obtain a particular sense of it as my home. I assure you that the love one then feels for the earth is intense; its composite spiritual entity is revealed and felt—and most curious and beautiful and varied it is."

Paulina smiled and shook her head. "Tom, I can't help doubting whether *I* should feel much affection for it. Besides, I think I prefer to think of myself not as an earth-creature, but as an individual spirit standing in a direct relation to God—if there is a God."

"I believe that we do also have such a relation too," said Wentworth, "but that relation is to me very obscure—a very deep mystery. I come nearest to apprehending it by meditating upon the eternal or archetypal forms." He fell into silence, and when next he spoke it was with a change of tone. "Let us go back to the subject of loneliness. When you were in the forest just now you ought not to have felt it to be indifferent or lifeless or alien. The fault lay in you; you had cut yourself off. One cannot feel lonely or meaningless when one feels that one is a part of the life around one."

Paulina answered with a sigh, and after a pause he went on: "During the years of my marriage to my first wife, Milly, I often felt my existence to be appallingly meaningless—which indeed in a sense it was. But I now see that its meaning was to have none—that is to say, it served me well by giving me an experience of meaninglessness acute enough to teach me once and for all how indispensable meaning is. Your married life similarly has been useful. Many people live meaninglessly all their lives without knowing it. The external life *is* meaningless, however busy and virtuous it is, unless it teaches you something."

"What about your second marriage? Was that meaningless, too?"

"My marriage to Rosita—no. And if you ever marry Stephen——"

"Marry Stephen? What do you mean?" interrupted Paulina with startled vehemence. "How can I marry him? There is no question—there can't ever be any question—of that. But go on about Rosita."

"I met Rosita in a suburb of Havana in the spring of—I forget. Anyhow it was about six years after my divorce from Milly. Rosita was leaning against the pillar of the veranda of her little house, doing nothing. The veranda was wreathed in sky-blue convolvuluses. Rosita was dressed in white muslin; her face was the most beautiful I have ever seen; she was seventeen, and her figure was exquisite. I stared, but walked on. How could I do anything else? However, on a door not twenty yards away—I should tell you that it was a street of small detached houses, each with a bit of garden—I saw a brass plate bearing the name Dr. A. J. Macgregor. I went in at once, consulted the doctor for sleeplessness, made myself as agreeable as I could, and finally invited him to dinner. Before dinner was over he had promised to introduce me to Rosita. I married her a fortnight later."

"You are rather impulsive, aren't you?" said Paulina, smiling.

"No, not really. I was ripe for something like that. The marriage itself presented no difficulties. Rosita's father was dead; her mother, a Creole, was a fat, lazy woman who looked as if she might have a tinge of native blood. The colour of Rosita's skin was indescribably lovely; her face seemed to shine with a cool, clear, inner, dusky light of its own. I still look upon it as a miracle that someone had not married her already, although she had only been out of her convent for nine days. Several young men of the district were after her, but none of them could settle five thousand dollars on her, besides a present of five thousand to her mother—which I was quite ready to make. Moreover, she herself liked Americans—that is to say, fair men; and my hair wasn't grey in those days. She was very innocent, and had hitherto taken very little interest in sex. But about a week after our marriage that changed.—I cannot really count my marriage to Rosita a mistake, a waste of life, for it was through her that I learned what an intense—an almost ecstatic—delight sheer physical passion can be. And now, do you know, often when I wander about under the trees my love and admiration for this earth are greatly heightened by the thought that it is the home of such passion—that the earth has, as it were, created such experiences. Whatever may be found on other planets, the love-passion which we earth-creatures know must assuredly partake of the uniqueness of the earth itself.—But to go back to Rosita: on our wedding tour we went from one island to another; and very soon I noticed something peculiar in the way her glance would slide over the young men we came across—especially fair, white-skinned young men. Little by little I came to realize that when she looked at a man like that she was wondering—she was thinking of him as a lover. I now feel pretty sure that Rosita was unfaithful to me even on our honeymoon, but, although I was jealous, I found that the distastefulness of keeping watch and guard over her all the time was more powerful than my jealousy—to say nothing of a kind of pride that always stood in my way. After a very short time it was borne in upon me that an exclusive preoccupation with sex is exceedingly boring. I am prepared to admit that it is more admissible, more entertaining, and more various than most monomanias; but it *is* of a boring monotony in the long run. Well, our trip ended at Pontchartrain, where I had some business to attend to; and there, as you know, the climax came. My unreasoning jealousy sprang out of my unreasoning physical passion. When I killed your uncle I knew exactly what I was doing; I was quite cool; but I was mad.

"All my passion for Rosita went out quite suddenly after that. During my two years in prison your father looked after her—and he continued to be extremely kind up to the day of her death. I felt sorry for what I had done, although your uncle was not a nice man in any way. He was singularly unlike your father.

"The birth of her child made no difference to Rosita; men remained her passion. When it became clear to both your father and me that nothing could change her, we let her live by herself and go her own way. A few years later she fell in love with a man who would have nothing to do with her, and then she drank herself to death. It was her way of committing suicide. As for Caroline, while I was in prison your father used to come and consult with me about her, and after my release he and I acted jointly as her guardians. He settled some money on her; she still has about four thousand dollars a year of her own. We sent her to a convent school, where she remained until she was eighteen. Just about that time your father died, and I took her to live with me. Yes, for about three months she occupied the room you are now occupying; on that day, eight years ago, when you first came here and saw me sitting upon that log, Caroline was here in this house.

" Well, although she was not bored here—she is of too passive a nature to become bored—I felt that marriage was her vocation and that it was my duty to give her a choice. So I travelled about with her, and it was on shipboard that she and Stephen met. Stephen was returning from a scientific expedition; he had been photographing a solar eclipse with the object of testing the truth of Einstein's theory. They became engaged in a very short time, and Stephen accompanied Caroline and me back here. I liked Stephen very much and felt bound to point out to him that he was taking a risk in marrying someone as intellectually limited as Caroline; but of course he paid no attention to me. He did right, for he was in love. Caroline was in love, too."

" And she still loves him," said Paulina in a low voice.

Wentworth considered. " Did Stephen imply that? Well, I suppose . . ."

After a pause he went on: " I may seem unfeeling in the way I speak of Caroline, but I must say what I believe to be the truth. I don't think she takes much interest in anything but her own wonderful beauty. Not even Matthew seems to mean very much to her. I say this because——"

" Tom," interrupted Paulina in a trembling voice, " please stop. I *have* learnt something in these last two years; and I'm not going to do any more harm. Tom, you must help me. There are only five days more before Stephen goes away. Let me stay here all the time—in this house with you. And if Stephen comes, will you talk to him for me, and send him away? You and he and Caroline and Matthew—you all belong together. I am an outsider. Surely you see that I am right?"

Wentworth looked troubled. " My dear, I want to help you. But how can I be sure you are right? If Stephen comes and talks to me, perhaps he will make me feel that *he* is right. How can I promise you anything?"

" Then I had better go away," said Paulina with a kind of contained violence. " I didn't come here for this. But go where?" And, bending forward, she buried her face in her hands. " I must go away," she repeated. " That was what I was thinking out there in the forest."

" No," said Wentworth, " you are mistaken. I feel sure you mustn't go."

There was an interval of silence.

"God knows I didn't come here for this," repeated Paulina in a muffled voice.

"How should *you* know what you came for?" said Wentworth with what seemed to be a touch of anger. "Do you really believe that you make your own destiny?"

Paulina lifted her head to look at him. Her cheeks were wet—her eyes wide and steady.

"However, in this case," continued Wentworth a little stiffly, "I think I can find *one* meaning at least in your coming. You came here for me—for my happiness."

Paulina's face changed; her gaze became more intent.

"You don't really mean that?" she pronounced after a moment. "You are saying it because . . ."

"Yes, I do mean it."

Paulina rose and stood by the bed. "You are kind. Your words are comforting." She looked down with a melancholy smile. "Dear Tom, if it really gives you pleasure, then of course my coming here has a meaning."

"No. Don't misunderstand me. I said a great deal more than you imply." The face which he turned up to her had a certain grimness. "I need you very much. Do you understand?"

"I—I don't think I do—not quite."

He hesitated; then gave a little laugh, and put his hand on hers. "You give me happiness, my dear, at a time when I need it. You give me something largely in excess of what a man has a right to expect."

"Oh, Tom!" exclaimed Paulina, and her eyes filled with tears. "I can hardly believe you. You can't really mean that!"

He nodded. "I do."

Paulina turned round abruptly, went to the open door, and stood looking out into the night.

When she came back she said: "If I am a blessing to you, you indeed are a blessing to me. And for as long as I can feel certain that I am adding something to your life I shall be satisfied."

Wentworth smiled. "Oh, but I don't want you to depend only on that. Do you remember, when you first came to this place years ago, it wasn't *me* you were looking for."

"I am not sure," said Paulina.

VI

AFTER leaving Paulina Stephen had walked quickly back to his car and driven off at top speed. His mind was filled with confusion and dismay; he was unable to understand what had happened. Why had this evening been so different from the last? Not for a moment had he doubted that it was going to carry him forward—a step nearer to an ultimate happiness. But now—before he had fully realized what was taking place—the evening had come to an end; they had said good-night; and something in the manner of their parting had seemed to take away all promise, all assurance, for the future.

As he drove furiously along the dark road, out of his bewilderment and despair an idea gradually emerged. "Yesterday evening we were just ourselves. We gave no thought to our connexions with other people, our respective settings. We forgot that we were not alone in the world. Each saw the other in freedom and isolation, and isn't that the way that human beings ought to come together? But this evening the world closed in round us. She got me to talk about my outward circumstances; she saw me and herself in relation to the world. She thought about people's opinions. Women are always servile to the world and to circumstance. They forge chains for themselves and others. They live in an entangling web of concern for appearances and public opinion—to say nothing of family life."

Stephen stopped his car by the roadside, and, still sitting at the wheel, pursued with increasing misery this line of thought. "Yes! yesterday evening she saw *me*—just *me*. This evening she saw, first, a lecturer—a man wrapped up in tiresome things that she couldn't understand—a pedagogue, a cog in the machine of a university. Then, as I talked, she saw a man exiled in a dreary, remote Russian town; she saw a man married, a man with a wife and child. She lost sight of *me*, of Stephen, altogether. But what the hell do any of these things matter? I needn't live in Russia. I can be divorced. But she *wanted* to lose sight of me, to bury me under entangling circumstances. That was her timid cunning; it was her wish to escape. If I had seized her, if I had taken her, that first evening, she would be mine now. But I have lost her. Now that I love her a hundred times more than ever, she has slipped out of my hands."

In agony Stephen sprang from the car and fell to pacing up and down the road. On both sides were dark, empty fields. He went up and down, up and down, unaware of his surroundings. In his mind's eye he saw the restaurant of the evening before; he re-created the scene, the people dancing, the little table at which they had sat; and Paulina herself—her dress, her hair, her face—she became poignantly real to him. He remembered the warmth and excitement of their growing intimacy, and the feel of her body as they danced together. Was that all finished? The exquisite promise of that evening, had it all melted away? And why?

His agony became so great that he opened his mouth and drew in the air in great gasping sobs. He longed to break out into howls and cries; he longed to roll in the dust and fill the night with the sound of his pain and rage. Clenching and unclenching his hands, he looked about for something to take hold of—something to clutch and break and tear. Finally, he went back to the car, leant his arms against it, and laid his head against his arms. He set himself to recall moment by moment the evening that had just gone by. At what point had he begun to notice that Paulina's gaiety was a little forced? It was certainly not till after he had told her about his marriage. She had shown curiosity about Caroline; she had asked him a good many questions about Matthew. Then she had become very quiet. They had lingered over their coffee in a quiet which for him had been full of happiness, because it had seemed to him that they were drawing closer and closer all the time. So deeply had he been lulled into security that when she had said she was tired and asked to be taken straight back to Tom's house, he had complied with very little protest. It was not until they were walking along the forest path that he had become aware that she was withdrawing herself from him. Troubled, he had taken her into his arms, he had besought her to tell him what was wrong. But it was no use. She was lifeless. A violent resistance would have been better than such lifeless yielding. Nor did she really yield. She let him kiss her cheek, but not her lips. And before he had fully realized that they were parting, they had parted.

Once again Stephen began walking up and down the dark road. He could not desist from recreating in imagination the feel of her body against his while they were dancing; again he heard her say: " I am enjoying myself." After a while he went back to the car and got in. " My God, I am going mad," he thought. " This is raving madness. A few days ago I was sane and happy. Now I am mad."

Half an hour went by, during which he never once moved. At last he drew out a handkerchief and wiped his face, for the sweat was running down it. " No, this is not a temporary obsession," he was thinking. "And although the pain can't go on at this pitch, I shall remain marked for life. I shall never get back to where I was before. I shall never get over this."

There followed an interval of stupor, and then he found himself once more driving the car along the dark road. "What am I to do? What is there to do?" he was muttering. He saw no possibility of explaining himself to anybody, not even to Wentworth. "When one is mad, one is cut off. No one—excepting another creature in the same plight—can understand. Besides, what is there to understand? I want Paulina. I can't live without her. That's all there is to understand. But why can't I live without her? I don't know. Something drags at me. I have a terrible pain in the heart—a longing, a craving, an anguish. How can I think of other things with this pain going on? How can I sail in five days' time? That would mean leaving Pontchartrain in three days. I can't do it. And if I did get myself on to the boat, shouldn't I jump into the sea before reaching Yokohama? And if I did reach Yokohama, I should be taking the next boat back."

For a few moments he thought of Caroline and Matthew. He had a vision of his house at Kharkov. It all seemed very far away. "What is a man's life? Things happen to him one after another, and they are mostly quite tame, and he goes on. He introduces a certain coherence and meaning into his life through his work. My work on the fine-structure constant—that forms part of an enduring and expanding whole. It will go on. Matthew will perhaps go on with it. But what about me? Where is my future now? Something has happened to me that destroys everything."

The road was quite straight. It ran between flat, empty fields. There was no traffic. The air was warm and moist; on all sides it was dark. Presently, however, he did notice a few lights a little way off the road. Some scaffolding and a derrick outlined against the sky told him it was the new oil wells. He stopped, got out, and walked stumblingly towards the lights. In a shed under an arc-light some men in overalls were squatting over a piece of machinery. They grinned at him with a certain curiosity as he came up and he realized that his apparition at this hour required explanation. "My radiator leaks," he said. "Got any water?" And he handed round a packet of cigarettes.

Glad of an excuse to make a pause, the men fell to talking about their drill. He forced himself to listen, but every few moments his attention slipped, and the effort to keep it fixed

soon became intolerable. The air, too, was nauseating with
the stench of crude oil. "I can't stand this," he suddenly
decided; and after saying: "Well, I must be off. Good night,
everybody! Good night!" he began to walk rapidly away.

"Hi, Mister! what about that water?" someone shouted
after him with a laugh, and he had to return and take a canful
to his car. Angrily he poured the water out on to the road,
and then brought the empty can back.

. . . . . .

Half an hour later his car was again drawn up beside the
rough track. He sat still in his seat gazing down it and straining
his ears to catch any sound. What he expected to hear he could
not have said. At last, getting down from the car, he moved
slowly in the direction of Wentworth's house.

On reaching the edge of the clearing he stopped. The little
house was clearly visible in the starlight. There was no glimmer
from inside, and he was obliged to infer that Paulina and Wentworth were asleep. Their sleep seemed to cut him off from them
as completely as though a gulf lay in between; he stood gazing
at the house longingly, unable to approach.

At last, making a wide circle round it, he took the path to
the bayou, and then walked along the edge of the water. The
stars were reflected, but otherwise the bayou was hardly visible,
so completely did it melt into the dark. He had it in his mind
to go to Wentworth's glade; he had been there once or twice,
and the place attracted him. But it was on the other side of
the bayou, and he saw no way of getting across. Presently,
however, he came upon a fisherman's boat, and paddled himself
over the water. In the forest on the other side there was no
path; and, being without a torch, he could only move very
slowly through the trees. It was not long before he lost his
sense of direction, and, becoming suddenly aware that he was
very tired, he lay down in a ditch that was full of dry leaves;
and almost at once fell into a dreamlike state.

"The stars!" he said to himself. "The stars! I look up
at the stars. Distance—what is it? Has it any meaning for
spirit? For love are there any miles, are there any leagues, are
there even light-years? Is Paulina asleep? Is she far? Does
her sleep carry her further than that star? Do we—do we ever
—through the partition of the dimensions—hear a calling, a
rap-rapping on the prison walls? The prison-walls of Space
and Time, they hedge a little moment in. And there the spirit
gropes and listens, until—Where is Paulina now? Dreaming
what dreams? She is in the little house behind the trees; she

is in the little room that I know; her sleeping head lies on the pillow. Her body is curled up in that bed—the bed that I know. Myself, three nights ago, I was in that house and never a thought of Paulina in my head. Now I am here, needing her —and she not needing me. She has become a part of the indifference and cruelty of the world. In spite of those eyes. A lovely childishness is in her eyes—always. Oh, my beloved, why must you snatch yourself away? Why fly from me? Is love so common, so cheap that you think nothing of it? When at last, in the long, dark night of Space and Time, we have met, must we fly past each other into the dark once more? Don't you understand that something wonderful might happen, that the skies might blaze and a new star be born? But in this there is also death. I have often said to myself: With death waiting, is it worth while to love? But now . . ."

VII

WHEN she woke up the next morning Paulina lay still for a while, looking idly at the play of sunlight and shadow upon the wall opposite. In the background of her mind there was sadness, but in the foreground peace. Peace illuminated with a gentle light her pictures of the life that she and Wentworth were now going to lead together. She was astonished by the happiness that she found in the thought that he needed her. Never had Harry needed her; no one had ever really needed her. But to Tom she could bring—what had he said?—"something in excess" of what he had any right to expect of life. "That excess," she now thought, "is sometimes a necessity."

Presently, as she was dressing, she heard the mulatto girl come in to do the housework; and when, a little later, she herself was busy in Wentworth's room, the sight of his contentment made her cry out in her heart: "Isn't this enough? Oughtn't this to be enough?"

Just before breakfast was ready, abandoning her tasks, she ran down the veranda steps into the sunlight. It was a brilliant morning; the sky dazzled her as she turned her face up to it. She ran on down the path under the trees, and the forest was shining with a beauty it had never worn for her before. Wonderful was the slanting light that came in under the boughs, streaking the fawn-coloured ground with long shadows and gilding sumptuously the great tassels of pendent moss; wonderful against the blue of the sky were the thin lianas and leafless twigs that made a web to catch the gold in the air.

She turned back. The gawky young mulatto who was sweeping out the veranda had a crimson handkerchief tied round her small head, which she balanced indolently upon her long brown neck. Here, too, there was beauty.

At breakfast she and her companion were gay, and after the meal was over she continued to sit by his side. Her gaiety, it was true, soon faded away into pensiveness; but she was not unhappy—or rather, not merely unhappy. One could be, she reflected, both happy and unhappy at the same time. It was a comfort to her to remain sitting at Wentworth's side for the feeling of security that his presence gave her. At the back of her mind was the thought: "What if Stephen appears? What will happen and what shall I do?" As the minutes went by this preoccupation became more and more insistent, and then, just as she was expecting, she caught the sound of a footstep outside.

Turning quickly, she met Wentworth's eye, and her expression betrayed her.

"Oh come!" he said. "You're not frightened, are you?"

She sat still, waiting, her face now completely expressionless.

"Hullo, Stephen," said Wentworth, as the young man appeared in the doorway. "You're early, but we were half expecting you. Come in."

Looking from one to the other, Stephen frowned, and Paulina could see that he would have preferred not to find them together. After a moment he advanced and stood by the foot of the bed. His face, which never had much colour, was perhaps a shade paler than usual, but otherwise there was nothing out of the ordinary in his appearance.

He gave a bleak smile. "I am rather early, I know. But why not?" His eyes were fixed on Paulina. "You knew I would come. So why should I wait?"

Paulina had kept quite still. Her gaze continued to be steady and expressionless; and now, without answering Stephen, she threw a glance in Wentworth's direction and got up. "I am going to let you two have a talk," she said.

An angry light came into Stephen's eyes. He took a step which placed him between Paulina and the door. For a moment no one moved or spoke.

"I have just sent a cable to the Soviet Government to say that I am not leaving America yet." He uttered these words in a harsh voice, and continued to fix Paulina challengingly.

" My dear boy," said Wentworth, " I hope that won't get you into trouble."

Stephen made no reply, but all at once his face, as he looked at Paulina, softened. " What have *you* got to say? " he asked. Paulina's eyes had been raised to meet the challenge in his; she now lowered them, but still remained silent. In order to get to the door she had to go round the foot of the bed, and Stephen was standing in the way.

Gradually Stephen's face changed completely. " Paulina! I want you to come and spend the day with me." His voice was now low and appealing. " Paulina! I have my car ready. Come! " Turning to Wentworth, he added: " Tom, this is really important. Tell her to come."

" No, no! " said Paulina hastily. " I can't."

" Yes, you must come."

" No, Stephen. I want you to have a talk with Tom. I can't come. I can't do it."

Stephen gave an unhappy laugh. " You can't *not* do it. Paulina, you can't treat me like this."

" But what do you . . ." She broke off. " Well, we'll have a talk here—in this house—if you really wish it."

" No. I want you to come with me—to-day."

Paulina bit her lip, glanced at Wentworth and then gave a little laugh that was no less unhappy than Stephen's. " What am I to say? This is too absurd. We can't go on arguing like this—one on each side of Tom's bed. I want to go now, Stephen. Later, if you still feel inclined to talk to me, you'll find me outside."

For a few moments Stephen neither moved aside nor said anything; he was looking at Paulina intently, and his eyes shone with such a passionate tenderness that all her self-possession melted away. Gradually a flush spread over her face, she cast her eyes down, and when Stephen took a step towards her she shrank blindly back. With a sigh that was almost a groan Stephen checked himself and made way for her to pass. At once she slipped out of the room.

    .   .   .   .

" Well," said Wentworth, " perhaps you'll sit down now and tell me what all this is about. And I dare say you'd like some coffee or something at the same time. Have you had any breakfast? "

" No."

" I thought not."

Stephen sat down in Paulina's chair and absent-mindedly began to eat and drink what was left on the tray.

"Listen, Tom," he said. "I have cabled to Moscow asking for permission—I put it like that in order not to annoy them—to stay here for another three weeks. The real trouble is this: Am I or am I not a Soviet citizen? I made an application years ago, but nothing much seemed to come of it—and, changing my mind in the meantime, I let the matter drop. I still have my English passport, so I imagine I'm all right. But we'll see what they say to my cable. It's no use meeting trouble half-way."

"Half-way!" Wentworth smiled ironically. "You seem to me to have been going all the way lately."

Stephen looked up from his plate and grinned. "Do I? Well, I can't help myself." But into his eyes, as he looked into Wentworth's, there crept a shadow of anxiety. "You understand, don't you? I want you to get this quite clear."

Wentworth lit a fresh cigarette. "All right," he said at last. "But explain yourself. Go ahead."

Stephen pushed back his chair. "I don't know how much she has told you already. The position is this: I loved her at once, and told her so the night before last. Everything seemed all right. But yesterday evening she drew away."

"I'm not surprised. What the hell do you expect of her? What are you suggesting exactly? What are your ideas for the future?"

"Tom, you know quite well that details must look after themselves. Don't be sticky. I know you too well."

"I'm not sticky. But let me tell you this plainly; one of the things she has on her mind is your family—Caroline and Matthew; and the sooner you——"

"Why, of course! Do you suppose I haven't been thinking about that all the time? But Caroline, as you know, doesn't care about me—not in a way that really matters. Actually Caroline doesn't present any great problem. Think of her beauty! There are hundreds of men ready to marry her and make her far happier than I can. Nor would she much mind giving Matthew up. He has never meant very much to her, you know. Perhaps you think Paulina will object to Matthew, but there you're wrong. I'm quite certain she'll get to like him. I bet you anything you like——"

"My God, you are a fool."

"Why?"

" Never mind why.—Go on."

" Well, as a matter of fact, fussing over all these details now *is* rather silly, but it was you who asked me to do it. The only practical point that bothers me is this: do those damned Russians look upon Matthew as a Soviet citizen? Will they make it difficult for me to get him out of the country? We may meet with trouble there. But never mind! I shall get him out somehow."

Wentworth considered Stephen with a reflective and sarcastic eye. " Why not take Paulina off to Russia with you? "

" I don't think she'd like it—not Kharkov anyhow."

" If you had her with you at Kharkov, *you* would be happy there, I suppose? "

" Of course I would. With her I should be perfectly happy anywhere. And for my special purposes the laboratory equipment in Kharkov is better than anywhere else. I could get ahead with my work quicker there than anywhere else." He paused, and then, watching Wentworth's face, added: " But you don't seriously think that Kharkov would be nice for Paulina; I'm sure you don't."

" Oh yes, I do," returned Wentworth, meeting Stephen's gaze with a smile. " If she really loved you, it would give her a good deal of satisfaction to think that she was making you happy in Kharkov—just Kharkov—with Matthew and the laboratory and all."

" Well," said Stephen slowly, " I'm not thinking of Kharkov for Paulina. I don't want that."

" Where do you want to live then? "

Stephen looked slightly uncertain. " My God! " he said at last. " What has come over you, Tom? This is worse than the Five Year Plan. As a matter of fact I should like to live *here*—in Pontchartrain. The laboratory is quite good; and, if I offer myself to these people, they won't refuse me."

Wentworth threw back his head and laughed. " My dear boy, it's no good. I know what's in your mind." He looked away, then added: " But I have several months before me, anyhow."

Stephen's whole manner suddenly underwent a change. " I am thinking of you, too. I admit it. Why not? Don't you suppose Paulina also will think of you—when we tell her? "

" I have asked you not to tell her—remember that. No need to—as yet."

Stephen paused; then, his face set, he leaned forward and

said: "Tell me, please, what was Hardy's report when you were last examined?"

"He said I might easily last another eighteen months."

"Oh, he said that, did he?"

"Yes."

Stephen's deep-set eyes were fastened upon Wentworth with a singular intentness. His brow grew dark; after a minute he got up and stood over him with an air that was almost menacing.

"Tom, you are being dishonest with me. It so happens that I was sent for by Hardy only the other day. He wanted to talk about you. He told me that, although eighteen months was possible, eighteen weeks was more likely, or—or even less, much less. He also told me very clearly that he had not held anything back from you; that you were the kind of man who had to be told the truth."

Wentworth's answer did not come at once. "Oh, very well!" He was looking slightly embarrassed. "What of it? I suggest that we talk about that some other time. Let's get back to your affairs. As I asked you before: What are your plans? What are your ideas for the future?"

Stephen looked surprised. "I want to marry Paulina, of course. I thought I'd said that. We are, as the phrase goes, made for one another." And he smiled.

"I think you're going rather too fast, my son. Things haven't come to that point yet."

"You mean . . ." Stephen grew sombre again. "No! But, by God, Tom, you've got to help me in this."

Wentworth tore open a fresh packet of cigarettes, lit one, and blew some smoke up at the ceiling. "I don't know. Frankly, I have to think not only of you but of her. How can I be sure that your breaking into her life like this . . ."

Stephen frowned and was silent.

"Damn it all!" exclaimed Wentworth with sudden warmth. "She has only known you—what? three or four days? And she came here to have a rest. She has just been through a pretty hard time. Now here you are, jumping on her out of the blue . . ."

Stephen got up and stood looking down at his companion. Nothing was said for a few moments.

"Oh, I know what you feel," the latter muttered at last, and he studied the palm of his hand.

Stephen remained silent.

"But you're going too fast all the same."

"Listen," said Stephen. "It is not likely—but it is just possible—that those Russians will answer my telegram in such a manner that I shall be forced to give up the idea of prolonging my stay here. They have a way, you know, of visiting the sins of the absent one upon his family. That's where they have me. I may be obliged to leave Pontchartrain in three days. And yet you tell me I'm going too fast."

Wentworth's face darkened. When he looked at Stephen again there was pity in his eyes.

Stephen cleared his throat and said: "I can't go back without feeling that Paulina is mine. I'm sorry, but I can't."

"Well, God help you!" said Wentworth.

Stephen turned and walked slowly out of the room.

VIII

PAULINA went down the veranda steps and stood still for some minutes as if in a dream. When she roused herself it was to move to the edge of the shade where an old hammock was suspended between two trees. Stretching herself out on it, she stared up into the dark foliage. "What shall I say to him when he comes? What shall I say?"

After a little her wandering thoughts took her back to England. She was at Bridgnorth again; it was a hot summer afternoon, the sun-blinds were down and all the house was quiet. She felt again the cool of her room, and smelt its clean, flowery smell . . .

Why did these memories invade her now? Why? when she ought to be thinking—thinking. Laying her hand over her eyes, she made an effort to concentrate. But on what? Her thoughts slipped away the moment she tried to grasp them. Her life, her present situation, the actual crisis, Stephen and Tom talking together in there—she couldn't focus upon them however hard she tried. And still Bridgnorth haunted her. She was again in her bedroom—a lovely room, pale blue, pale rose and grey, a room bathed in the flood of cool light that came in through the four large windows, beneath which spread an English countryside. She thought of that room with pleasure because it had beauty, but without any regret or even any liking. There had been one day that summer, when, lying on her sofa by the window, she had heard Harry's voice coming up from the terrace below. He was talking to Guy, and Guy suspected that Harry was beginning to suspect. The tone on both sides was one of false and careful friendliness, and she remembered what a strange, hard frame of mind she had been in; how she had said to herself with a shrug that she didn't really care what either of these men felt, or thought, or did. No, their feelings didn't matter to her. But even when not in that mood a deep-seated, hidden indifference seemed at that time to lie at the root of her life. "Yes," she said to herself, "the trouble was that I didn't love Harry—not even in the beginning."

There had been a period, perhaps, when she might have learnt to love him, only—his secretiveness and cunning stood in the way. To do herself justice, she *had* tried to get past that barrier, but without success; and little by little she had come to understand that on the other side of the barrier there was nothing she was really in sympathy with. "To think that three years of my life went like that!" she murmured to herself, and she turned over in her hammock with a moan of shame and pain.

Wentworth's little house was now before her eyes, and that she firmly loved. She gazed and gazed, and after a while she was imagining another little house quite near, a house where she would live. It would be over there—just out of the shade of that ilex, and she would stay there always. And perhaps Stephen would bring Caroline and Matthew to settle down in Pontchartrain, and she would become friends with them too. She wouldn't let Caroline feel any jealousy; she would make that impossible. As for Matthew—to love him, and to make him love her, that would surely come easily enough. So they would all be happy together, and the years would go by, and this would be her life.

Her eyes were closed and she was in this dream when a footfall on the veranda made her lift her head with a start. Stephen was coming down the steps, and after a moment of sick hesitation she swung her feet to the ground and went to meet him. To her dismay a sudden dizziness had seized her, but she fastened her eyes steadily upon Stephen and kept her face fixed in a smile. The landscape wavered, the ground rocked; but she managed to walk without stumbling. They met and paused. Stephen looked terribly concrete and real, and she felt a pang of dread. "Well!" She smiled up at him. "Well, you've had *your* talk with Tom, and now—now *I* want to talk to him for a minute. Will you try that hammock? It's deliciously comfortable.''

Stephen said nothing. He was looking at her with a gentleness that was full of anguish and supplication.

"I shan't be long." She spoke with nervous haste. "And afterwards, if you still want to, you can take me into Pontchartrain and we'll have luncheon at Celestin's.'' She stopped short suddenly. Had she really meant to say this?

Stephen's gaze was intent and yet absent. "My darling!" he said beneath his breath.

Paulina quivered and passed on.

Wentworth's room seemed dark and cool after the hot sunlight. She was thinking: "I mustn't confuse things. First of all, Caroline and Matthew have to be considered. Yes, those two first of all." She sat down by the bed and gave her companion a smile.

"You look rather white," he said.

She shook her head impatiently. "I lay in the sun too long—that's all." And she went on: "I have just said to Stephen that I would lunch in Pontchartrain with him. I can't refuse to talk things out. I can't just run away, can I?"

"No." Wentworth paused. "But please don't ask me to give you advice. There are two different ways of looking at this: and I don't know enough to decide . . ."

"Oughtn't you to think of the absent?" said Paulina. "Surely you ought to speak for Caroline."

"To Stephen or to you? Stephen may talk callously, but he isn't really callous."

"He may be mistaken about Caroline. She may feel—or she might feel—more than he thinks."

"That's possible. But even so . . ."

Paulina continued to sit upright, looking straight before her. Wentworth remained equally still.

At last with a certain abruptness she got up; and then, bending down, kissed Wentworth on the forehead. "Will you go on loving me however much I hurt Stephen—and myself?"

The other sighed rather wearily. "Yes—I will."

Paulina went out, walked along the veranda into her own room, and sat down on the bed.

"I don't seem to be any longer in the everyday world," she was thinking. "He has done *that* to me, at any rate." She looked round the room and felt frightened. Everything was alien, there was nothing that had not lost its familiar aspect. The room and the things in it seemed to say to her: "You are no longer the being we know. You stand outside, you are strange, you are separated." She wondered whether she ought not to be passive; she longed to accept the good and the bad in passivity. Was it right to take one's fate into one's own hands, when it made one feel so monstrous, so self-isolated?

"Is there nowhere that I belong?" she asked herself in anguish. "Why am I so imprisoned, so cut off, when I am only trying to do right? Why do I stand in a position which makes even Tom withdraw from me?" And loneliness again swept over her.

She went cautiously to the window and caught sight of Stephen leaning against a tree at the edge of the clearing. Once, for a moment, she thought she heard Wentworth calling her, and her heart leapt up with joy; but it was evidently a mistake, for as she stood listening she heard nothing more.

She began to tremble and felt so weak that she went back to sit on the bed. "How terrible to think that the days, the weeks, the years, that are to come depend upon what I do now. Shall I look back upon this decision of mine with horror and regret? And yet, if I yield, what will the future do to me? Shall I not be taking upon myself equal responsibility? and very likely a load of even greater pain?"

She forced herself—not without a sense of futility and unreality—to plan her conversation with Stephen; she considered what arguments to use, what devices to employ for mitigating the pain that she was about to inflict. She pictured herself and Stephen walking down through the wood to his car. There wouldn't be time then to embark on anything serious; nor on the way into Pontchartrain; but at Celestin's it would be best to begin almost at once. "Will he reproach me?" she cried, within herself. "Will he say that I am to blame? Will he feel bitter as well?" That, she felt, would be more than she could bear. And yet—was she to blame? Was she?

Pressing her palms against her forehead, she started up from the bed. "If I stay here any longer I shall become hysterical." After drinking a glass of water, she picked up her hat and dust coat and left the house.

The sun and air did her good, and as she went up to Stephen she succeeded in smiling quite naturally. With a gesture he invited her to go before him along the little winding path, but before they had taken more than a few steps he stopped her and made her look back at the house.

" Do you remember three days ago how frightened you were when you saw me alone in the veranda, and thought that Tom had died? "

" Three days ago! " murmured Paulina, wonderingly. " Yes."

" A good deal has happened to us since then."

She made no reply.

" There is now a bond."

Paulina still kept silent; but the truth of his words struck down straight to her heart. Yes, there was a bond. She walked on—very slowly, because she felt so uncertain. Time seemed to have broken up; it repeated itself, its sequence was lost. Now! Eight years ago! Three days ago! These occasions were all mixed up. She had a vision of her mother waiting for her in the sitting-room of the hotel; in the evening the music of the pleasure-boat would come wailing in through the window. Her mother, Rupert, her old nurse Marthe, Harry— their shades drifted past her. A longing for bygone things caught at her heart, and that longing was joined by an intense craving for peace.

" But most memories are only garments," she thought. " They don't get stamped upon the substance of one's being. They are garments that become ragged, and flutter, and are lost upon the wind. Only now and again do eternal moments touch one; as light as a butterfly perhaps, and quite simple and quiet in their coming. Yet those moments are like thunderless lightning, and pierce secretly to the core."

Stephen had put his arm through hers, and she knew that *this* was one of her " eternal moments." She said to herself: " He will be with me in memory for ever. Then how can a severance be made? How can a severance be right? "

They got into the car.

" My darling," said Stephen, " I am not going to take you to Pontchartrain. We are going down towards the Gulf."

IX

SHE woke from her musings to find herself passing through country that she had never seen before. The sun, now high overhead, was shining fiercely through a white haze. Fields of short, greyish grass bordered the road, and behind there rose clumps of huge, moss-hooded trees, the outposts of a line of forest. In the chalky, violet sunlight these mountainous forms loomed up hollow and spectral; they looked like lumps of foam left by a withdrawing tide. And the forest behind seemed to be more unsubstantial still—hoary and unsubstantial with an ancientness independent of time. A frontier of mystery, it stretched on for mile after mile; always the same distance away, it tantalized Paulina until suddenly the road made a turn, and the car rushed into it and was engulfed. At once a cool, swampy smell filled the air; pools of water glittered in the half-dark, the car plunged through clouds of noise that came from the throats of countless frogs.

After a while Stephen said: " Are you getting tired? We shall soon be there."

Paulina turned her head. " Where? "

He smiled. " You'll see. We are going as far as one can go by road. To go further one must have a boat."

" And if one has a boat? "

" One goes on and on through forest and marsh, and gradually the bayous become broader and banks of white sand appear. The water gets clearer, the land melts away, and at last you are on the Gulf."

A little later Paulina noticed that the forest was becoming less dense, and soon the road was running along in sight of a broad, winding waterway with little tumble-down shacks upon its grassy banks. At last a group of houses appeared, and Stephen said: " Here we are."

Beyond the houses for as far as the eye could see there stretched a marsh, russet and silver in the sunlight. On the right of the road there glittered the broad waterway with broken forest beyond.

Stephen drew up before a two-storied wooden house and jumped out of the car. " Wait a minute," he cried, and ran down to the water's edge to hail a man who was sitting in a boat. Paulina heard them talking together in French, and when he came back he was looking pleased. " Pierre will take us out after luncheon. It was great luck finding him; he's just back from the Gulf. A nice man—you will like him."

" He looks nice," said Paulina.

" Catching shrimps and musk-rats is his job. It's a beautiful life. You'll see."

" Shall I? " said Paulina, smiling.

" I mean, he'll tell you about it."

A girl appeared from the restaurant, bringing two large

tumblers of red wine. "Good morning, Marie!" cried Stephen. "I see you know what we want. But we must also have something to eat soon."

"I have some lovely gumbo," said the girl, looking shyly at Paulina.

Paulina's face fell.

"Madame doesn't like gumbo," laughed Stephen. "Anything but that."

"Stuffed crab?"

"That will do."

"And chicken?"

"Better still! Don't you think so, Paulina?"

"Yes." She got out of the car, feeling happy. And she saw that Stephen was feeling happy too. He had become aware that she was happy before she herself had realized it.

"Drink your wine," he said.

"It tastes rather odd, doesn't it?"

"Yes. But it doesn't do one any harm. I've drunk lots of it, haven't I, Marie?"

"*Mais oui*," agreed Marie, smiling with pride, while to Paulina she said reassuringly: "Monsieur is right. It does one no harm."

"Hurry up with the crab and the chicken," said Stephen, and, thrusting his arm through Paulina's, he took her along a little footpath that ran by the waterside. It was a narrow path of pale brown mud and the twisted roots of water-cypresses and palmettos made it very uneven. They went along slowly, enjoying the cool of the air which seemed to Paulina to smell faintly of the sea. The olive-green water lapped at the steep bank of mud on one side, on the other was a rickety fence, enclosing empty gardens that backed a row of small wooden houses. In the broad gaps between the houses the marsh was visible, its grasses blowing silvery in the wind. A faint blur here and there on the horizon marked the edge of the forest beyond.

They had not gone far before Paulina drew Stephen to a halt. "Look!" she said. "Hen-run and private cemetery combined."

They were standing outside some wire-netting that enclosed a small patch of ground over which there wandered a score of dejected fowls. In the centre of this dirty mud-patch the outline of two graves was visible; one of them, plainly of recent origin, being decorated with bits of broken glass. As they stood there

silent, a boy of about ten entered the run from the other side.
He was pale brown like the mud, ill-nourished and vacant-eyed.
In one hand he had a large tin, in the other a bunch of fading
flowers. The fowls rushed towards him in a scampering, flut-
tering mob and threw themselves upon the contents of the tin
as he emptied it on to the ground. Kicking them aside with
his bare feet the boy advanced to the new grave and laid his
flowers down inside the half-circle of broken glass. Scarcely
had he done so before the hens, their brief repast ended, rushed
back and attacked the flowers with an almost equal voracity.
Snatching them up in their beaks, they scattered rapidly over
the run to devour this dessert at their leisure. It was in vain
that the boy kicked and beat at them; in a few moments the
grave was as bare as it had been before.

Not until after he had actually engaged in combat with the
fowls did he catch sight of Stephen and Paulina, and then it
was too late to stop. After his defeat he stood and looked at
them with a face every muscle of which was twitching. Was he
going to cry or could he manage a laugh? Stephen and Paulina
at once began to laugh; they pointed at the hens with contempt.

" *What* silly creatures! " cried Paulina. " Just look at them!
Don't they look silly? "

" Yeah," said the child, a smile just breaking through.

" Poor things! they're hungry, and they know no better."

The boy began to laugh and suddenly flung his tin at two hens
who were disputing over the largest of the flowers. " God-
darned fools! " he said.

" Here," said Stephen, and he held out a half-dollar.

The boy took it, and the two went on.

After a moment Paulina said: " Do you know, I think that
we—all of us—are almost equally piteous."

" Yes," said Stephen, and he added: " But it doesn't seem
to matter."

" No," said Paulina, " it doesn't really matter."

They smiled.

.   .   .   .   .

After luncheon she sat on the bank, and while Stephen and
Pierre were preparing the boat, she examined herself anxiously.
" What is the meaning of my present frame of mind? On what
does it rest? Is it really me? Is it true? Is it deep? " The
answer came that she was being completely herself, and true
to herself. But it was strange; never in her life before had she
been so conscious of being a self-determining creature, and yet

now, so far as she could judge, she was letting go, letting herself drift as passively as those detached water-lily leaves that were drifting down the stream. "We think of moods as if there were times when we were not in any mood at all. But the most detached philosopher in his most detached moment is as much in a mood as somebody who is in love. By what criterion is one to judge of moods? Of course in some moods more than in others we are likely to do things that we may afterwards regret. But what of those illumined moods when even regret and the fear of regret are despised? What of them?"

Rising to her feet, she took the hand that Stephen was holding out to her and stepped down on to the little deck that covered the bows. At once the boat began to move down the water-way, and she stretched herself out at full length, her chin upon her folded arms, the olive-green water rippling away beneath her, the sun warm on her back. "This is another world," she thought, "a far-away world that is like a world after death."

Happy, she watched the strange landscape sliding past. On the bank hoary trees shimmered in the silvery light. Small black cows stood in the water, head and back alone emerging, as they munched at the hog-grass that grew among the water-lilies. Great banks of water-lilies, so solid that the boat had to skirt round them, made islands in the placid stream. Now and then a little desolate shack appeared, with a rude pier belonging to it, and a small boat alongside. Paulina saw these things and yet did not see them, for somehow she and the outward scene had fused into one. How feeble and dilute was the sense of actuality that one got in ordinary life, how weak one's habitual apprehension of the wonder of the living Now!

She looked at Stephen, who was outstretched beside her. "It is through him, through my love of him, that this immediacy and intensity come to me," she thought; and Stephen, as he looked back at her, suddenly said: "I am happy. But tell me, my beloved, I am not behaving wrongly in your eyes, am I?"

She smiled. "Sometimes, I suppose, the present *may* be cut off from the past and the future. Sometimes, I think, sometimes."

He began to consider her reply. In reality the past and the future were not cut off. All his past and all hers—their infancy, the days of their youth, all the years that lay behind them, had contributed to the making of this present moment. In the landscape of their Here and Now their past might be likened to the solid earth, while the future, or rather their prevision of it, was like the arch of heaven hanging above and imparting to the landscape its light, its colour, its significance and intensity.

He said: "What we have done is only to throw off the oppression of the past and the fear of the future." Putting an arm round her shoulders, he looked into her face and laughed exultantly. "In those—in those alone is the sting and victory of Time. My darling, I feel that in throwing those off we become as gods."

Her smile was full of love. "Even while we still remain like that small boy, piteous?"

"Yes."

. . . . .

A little later, Stephen got up, gave a call to Pierre and pointed to the left. Pierre altered his course, and the boat entered a narrower waterway, both banks of which were overshadowed by tall trees. It was cooler here where the shade fell over the water, but the trees on the right-hand bank were lit by the westering sun, and the gloom of the forest behind was slashed by vistas of light.

Stephen, leaning against the cabin-wall, looked down for a while upon the figure of Paulina, then he turned and went into the cabin. He knew this cabin well, for Pierre had often shown it off to him with pride. "Look at the stove, a fine stove on which one can cook well. Here one can wash; and there——" he would point to a broad divan—"it is there I sleep. Ah! but that is a good place to sleep—better far than my bed at home." There was something very agreeable about both Pierre and his cabin; they were clean, comfortable, civilized. Stephen now went round the cabin, examining this and that, and sniffing contentedly. The place was full of faint smells, all of which were clean and agreeable. He picked up the coverlet of musk-rat skins upon the couch; it was deliciously soft; and smelt good. "Like the top of a dog's head," he thought.

Leaving the cabin he went to the stern, where Pierre was steering.

"You've got some traps laid somewhere near here, I think. Would you like to have a look at them?"

"It'll take me at least a couple of hours to walk round."

"I don't mind. Put in under that bank."

As the noise of the engine died away and the boat glided slowly to a standstill, Paulina roused herself and sat up. The great wall of trees opposite was glowing ruddily, and she lifted her face with pleasure to the reflected heat and light. Under the tall ilex where the boat now lay the air was cool and damp. Here one smelt the smell of the water which was neither the sweetly dank smell of rivers nor the salty smell of the sea, but a mixture of both. And the smell of the land was in the air, too—a smell of forest and sun-heated swamp.

She rose to her feet, and, looking over the roof of the cabin, saw Pierre with a sack on his back stepping out on to the bank.

" Good luck to you," said Stephen, and Pierre, after grinning and waving his hand, was lost among the trees.

Silently Paulina sank down upon the deck again. For a few moments she heard no sound. The silence was deep. She held her breath, and when her respiration started again it was short and quick. Stephen was now to be heard coming forward towards her. In another minute he was bending over her and drawing her up on to her feet. Gathering her into his arms, he pressed her body against his. Then he picked her up off her feet and carried her into the cabin.

. . . . . .

The sun was just setting as the boat moved slowly back over the iridescent water. While the dove-coloured sky above gradually darkened, the glassy surface of the bayou seemed still to retain its light. Where the arrowy wave from the bows spread outwards to the greying banks the light on that smooth undulation passed through all the tints of a lunar rainbow. Tender and mournful and strange did the fall of the night seem to Paulina as she lay on the still-warm deck. No lights burned in the little houses on the banks; there was no movement in all the silent landscape; the ragged outline of the trees against the sky was absolutely still.

PART III

I

THE great level of the Mississippi Delta, grassland and swamp and forest, was growing grey with dusk. Wide and high above it a level ceiling of delicate cloud caught the sunset's tints, and throwing them down upon bayou and lake, inlaid the plain with traceries of light. More faintly did the long white roads pattern the grey—roads upon which the rushing cars, like little comets, swept their tails of dust. Across ten empty miles Pontchartrain, studded with lights, rose angular and glittering before Stephen's eyes. He was driving as one asleep; behind him were Wentworth and Paulina; all three were silent with the silence of the regions where they had spent their day.

" To-night," thought Wentworth, " to-morrow and to-morrow night—for them no more is left. But for me—how much remains? No one can tell. A summer, a winter, and another summer? Certainly not more."

He gave a glance at Paulina by his side. She noticed it and smiled at him, then closed her eyes. " She is pale," he thought, " she is tired."

" Put your head on my shoulder," he said. " It has been a long day."

She obeyed, and presently she seemed to be asleep, for her weight against him became inert; but at the next bend of the road he was startled, for she began to slide down from the seat. Thrusting an arm round her, he drew her up again, then he leant forward and tapped Stephen on the shoulder.

Stephen glanced round, drew up at the side of the road, and got quickly down from the car.

" Don't worry," said Wentworth. " She fainted like this only a week ago; and I feel certain it's not serious. I said nothing about it, because she was anxious that I shouldn't."

In the half-light Stephen looked haggard. He bent down and peered closely into Paulina's colourless face.

" It may last ten minutes or more," the other continued. " Let us take her into that field out of the dust."

Together they carried Paulina a little way off from the road and laid her down upon the dry short grass. Then they sat down and waited.

" But why? What is the matter with her?" Stephen muttered. " I wish you had warned me."

" The matter?" Wentworth frowned and looked away. " Everything is the matter. It can't be helped. But I think it's time that you and she . . ."

" Well?"

" I think it is time you stopped being so happy."

There was a silence.

" We haven't been pretending," said Stephen hoarsely. " We *are* happy."

" I know you are."

Again there was a silence.

" It's an odd thing certainly," said Stephen. " We have become happier every day—right up to now."

" I know," said Wentworth helplessly. " That's all right."

" Is it mad?" asked Stephen with violence.

" No."

Together they stared straight before them across the level plain. " From the beginning," thought Stephen, " we have been marvellously happy, and our happiness instead of being strained and tense has become more carefree and light-hearted every day. We have laughed together. We have had fun together—and how *natural* it has all been. Why, we have even quarrelled—as if we had even time for that!"

His companion's voice broke the course of these thoughts.

" Tell me," Wentworth spoke in an undertone, " you haven't thought of another plan, have you? I mean, you haven't found an alternative?"

Stephen shook his head.

" Nor any change in the prospect?"

" No," said Stephen shortly. And then he added: " There is no alternative. I must go. I can't leave Caroline and Matthew there."

" And then?"

Stephen clenched his teeth. " Oh, I shall get them out. I shall come back with them—somehow."

After looking at him fixedly for a minute the other turned his head away.

Suddenly Stephen bent down and kissed Paulina over her closed eyes. When he drew back he found that her eyes were open and staring at him vacantly. " She's coming to," he said.

" Good." Wentworth took a flask from his pocket and

poured out some brandy. "In a few moments you can give her some of this."

. . . . .

Dusk had now settled more darkly upon the wide sweep of the plain, the air had become damper, a few stars were shining through the thin clouds overhead. Wentworth, Stephen and Paulina were gazing across the vague stretches before them to where the black mass of Pontchartrain towered and twinkled. Points and bars of emerald, ruby, and topaz light bejewelled it; and these sharp little fires dulled the rusty glow of the sunset behind. But on the city's western verge that glow was concentrated in a band of stronger light, and there the mournful, ragged outline of the swamp-forest was defined.

After a while Paulina stirred, turning her eyes to look at Wentworth whose head and shoulders were dark against the sky. "I think I know one of the reasons why you live here," she said.

"Why?"

"Because history and tradition get in your way, and here there is little of either."

Wentworth considered. "Perhaps you are right."

"My darling," said Stephen suddenly, and he bent over Paulina, whose head was resting against his shoulder. "Tom thinks we are both mad."

Paulina looked at Wentworth again and gave a little laugh. "Really, Tom! Have you been taking advantage of my fainting to say that?"

"No. I didn't say it."

"He said it was time we stopped being so happy."

Paulina paused before answering. "I don't think we *can* stop, so long as we are together. But anyhow . . ." she paused again, "anyhow, you don't really believe that to love is to be mad, do you?"

"No." Wentworth gave a shrug. "Very likely only lovers and ecstatics are sane."

"Are you an ecstatic?"

"By God, he is!" said Stephen.

Paulina laughed. "*Un mystique à l'état sauvage*—that's what you are, Tom."

Wentworth's eyes were still fixed upon the darkening skyline. "History, tradition, culture are all very well in their way; but they are not enough. What is history but the story of poor little men like ourselves? I want a vision of Man. When I look into the past I see a procession of people all in fancy-dress—the human spirit taken in by its own various make-believes. From that point of view there is very little to choose between the painted savage and Beau Brummel in satin. Manners maketh Society, not Man.—But I am speaking only for myself. I know what I am after. And history doesn't help me—or, at any rate, only illustratively."

" Then what does help you? Science?"

" Not as providing anything positive; but as a deliverance, yes. To think about atoms and stars is a deliverance. Science throws history into its right place. It takes one out of the cathedrals, picture-galleries and museums into the starry night. But a purely scientific approach to what I want is no more practicable than a historic approach."

" Please explain then. What is it that you want?"

"I don't know. Perhaps—fulness of life."

These last words took Paulina a little by surprise, and she fell silent. Leaning her head once more against Stephen's shoulder, she closed her eyes.

" Yes," Wentworth continued after a moment, " to throw off the shams and trivialities that cramp and stifle life—that is what we need. And another way of putting it would be this: I want a vision of Man. I want to perfect my vision of the archetypal forms of the human spirit. I want to see Man and Woman and Childhood and Adolescence and Old Age, as Blake, for instance, saw them; and still more I want to discern the forms of Joy, Courage, Mercy, Love, Innocence and Wisdom, as in their essence they are." He paused, then added in another tone: " But I expect all this sounds rather woolly."

"No, Tom," said Stephen. " I don't think your intuitions are woolly. It's your inferences that I can't always follow."

Wentworth laughed and rose slowly to his feet. " Oh well, so long as you agree that the worldling's vision of the world is no truer than Blake's or Traherne's!"

" I'm sure he agrees," said Paulina. She opened her eyes and sat up. " But—can one *always* see the corn as ' orient and immortal wheat, which never should be reaped, and was never sown '? Tom, I do wish one could."

Wentworth stood looking down at her, and she could tell in spite of the darkness that there was a smile upon his face. " Listen!" he said. " Here is another passage, my dear, which ought to please you: ' Suppose a curious and fair woman. Some have seen the beauties of Heaven in such a person. It is

a vain thing to say they loved too much. I dare say there are
ten thousand beauties in that creature which they have not
seen.'"

Paulina laughed, but a little tremulously.

" I think Traherne is right," said Wentworth. " Lovers add
beauty to the world."

" They add life," said Stephen, " intensity to life."

" And unhappiness," murmured Paulina.

" Yes." Wentworth paused for a moment. " In two days'
time you will both, I suppose, be very unhappy. But in that,
too, there will be beauty." And, turning away, he began to
walk slowly back towards the road.

II

THE next day dawned with a slow, warm wind blowing from the
Gulf, blowing across the dead-smooth sea, sweeping the stars
from that floor of glass, sweeping up long, low wavelets to
ripple over the white sand-bars. Swaying the boughs, swinging
the moss, over the forest it came, and it filled the white curtains
in the window and lifted Paulina's hair on the pillow, lifted and
blew, lifted and blew, brushing her hair against her cheek until
at last she woke.

" A wind," she thought, " a hot wind, like the one that blew
over the Gulf. When we bathed the water was rippling—and
full of sunlight right down to the white sand. The smell of the
narcissus-fields was carried out over the sea; we lunched in the
shade of an ilex by the shore—and all that day I knew I was
loved. We came home in the dusk, we drove into the sunset—
and I knew I was loved. And that evening, while he lay beside
me, the hot wind rustled the window-curtain, and my hair blew
into my face, and gradually he fell asleep. And I, lying awake,
thought: ' I will remember this.' "

She watched the sunlight dancing on the wall, and other
moments, other scenes, drifted past her. Then, after a while,
raising herself on one elbow, she looked at Stephen. " He will
wake soon; and then we shall both be thinking: This is our
last day!—but a kind of happiness will well up in us in spite
of it."

The hot wind gathered strength as the hours went by; clouds
gathered and flew rapidly overhead. In the afternoon Paulina

left the house and wandered off alone. It was not her intention to go far, but when she found herself upon the road with the wind in her face a desire for movement took possession of her. Her eyes fixed upon the ground, she went forward mechanically. "After he is gone," she thought, "I shall still have Tom. And Tom, for as long as he lives, shall have me. There is no struggle, no conflict, in this. To leave Tom is unthinkable. But while he is dying, what is my life to be? I suppose that what I give and what I receive—that must suffice me. I shall have to thrust the thought of Stephen down, down, out of the light. I shall have to thrust my heart down into an oubliette. All that is most alive in me, all that I hold dearest—underground, underground! One has a living happiness, a happiness that wants to laugh and dance under the sun, and one must bury it. It is banished into the past—and

> ' There its beauty makes
> That vault a feasting presence full of light.' "

She walked on. " Sometimes I shall visit that vault—just to keep my heart alive. Otherwise in the long drag of unecstatic days I shall fail, and fall, and sink. There will be times when the flame is almost flickering out, times when everything is nothing, the world not even a mystery."

As she pushed on against the wind she felt in her heart the first real pangs of the coming separation. This was the suffering which she had been building up for herself during the last three weeks. With what a strong, subtle determination she had laboured towards this end—the greatest possible love, the greatest possible pain. She had put all her energies into the enrichment and adornment of it. It was *their* love, *their* pain— and she had forced Stephen to join in its building up. Why had she done this? Had it been a folly or a sin?

There was no regret or repentance in her mind, but only wonder. Stephen and she might go their ways and never meet again, but here in the forest, in the wilderness, their love had its secret shrine. To this place their memories would travel back, wailing round the idol of this love, always longing, always unappeased.

" I shall never repent, I shall never regret," she said to herself, " no, never ! " And yet she was also remembering how Stephen had said that there was something almost devilish in the way she had spun her threads about his heart, leaving no part of it free. In a little while he would be standing by himself on the ship, haggard, brooding, looking back over the grey water. Looking back towards their love, looking back into the past; seeing once again the ragged outline of the swamp-forest and glassy surface of the bayous where they had been so happy. She took pleasure in thinking that he would hold himself apart, shunning his kind lest he lose something of the still-lingering magic of her nearness. The little things she had given him would always be there under his hand; she had given them with the secret thought that they would remind him.

At this point the wind became so violent that she stopped and decided to turn back. She was standing on a lonely stretch of the road with a long line of forest not far away on her right. The whistling air seemed to be hurrying the whole landscape along with it: branches were tossing in a frenzy, the moss waved in long tattered streamers. " I wondered once whether I should ever see these trees in a gale," she said to herself, " these old King Lears, their beards plucked by the wind! "

As she was walking back she fell to thinking about a recent conversation with Wentworth. She had said to him: " How odd it is that while I foresaw the unhappiness that was to come and finally ceased to trouble about it, I never gave a thought to the happiness." And Wentworth had answered that love was reckless of happiness, and rightly. Its apparent fatalism sprang from the knowledge that it was an end in itself.

" How suddenly Stephen and Tom and I have been caught in the grip of Fate," she now thought. " We are puppets, piteous puppets. Tom must die. Stephen must go away. I must stay. And something tells me that I shall never see Stephen again. All this, measured in terms of happiness, is terrible; but there is another measure of things, I suppose—or perhaps another happiness? I must try to find it, and Tom will help me. I feel that in imagination he is able to share in the life of the earth as a whole. I sometimes feel him to be inhabiting not only his little house but all the great cities of America, aware of the desperation that is gripping the people like a black frost—and he is also upon the empty oceans, on the dusty Asian plains, and in the jungles of the tropic South. I feel him to be aware of the hungry, toiling populations of India, China, and Russia."

On the thought of Russia she lingered. With a painful clearness of vision she saw the snowy streets of Kharkov. She saw the little wooden house (Stephen had described it to her) where Caroline, indolent and beautiful, lay yawning before a white-tiled stove. In Kharkov it would be afternoon. The sun would be thawing the snow upon the roof, and Caroline no doubt was listening to the drip from the eaves.

Knitting her brows and closing her eyes, she pushed on against the wind. " No, no! It is too much! " she cried out in sudden pain. " I only want to be happy. Instead of trying to embrace the whole earth and all the stars, instead of holding the past and the future as well as the present in my brain, I want just to be happy as children are—happy in a tiny circle of immediate time and place." But she knew that retreat was impossible.

III

STEPHEN and Wentworth had been sitting in the veranda when Paulina wandered off, and they followed her with their eyes until she was lost among the trees. Her departure brought into their minds the thought that this might well be the last real talk they would ever have together, and there was a slight constraint in the sadness that came over them.

Wentworth leant forward to study the sky. " The rain will be coming soon; I hope she won't go very far."

" No; I don't suppose she'll go far."

" How does she seem? All right?"

" Yes, I think so."

Again they were silent, listening to the wind. It was roaring in the tree-tops, although the house itself, sheltered, lay in a little oasis of calm.

" Look here!" said Wentworth abruptly. " Have you thought any more about what I said to you last night?"

" What did you say?" muttered Stephen, although the question was unnecessary.

" I said that it was not too late yet for you to take Paulina with you."

" No, I haven't thought about it," returned Stephen, a note of anger in his voice.

" You must have," replied Wentworth.

" Well, if I did, it was only to reject the idea."

" All the same, you *must* listen to me now." Wentworth paused, his eyes resting upon Stephen gravely. " I want you to help me to persuade Paulina to go with you. Think! There is absolutely no reason why she shouldn't get into the train with you to-morrow morning and travel straight through to

Moscow. You would leave her there, I suppose, until you had come to an understanding with Caroline; then—well, then you would be guided by circumstances; but presumably you would aim at getting away from Russia with all three of them— Caroline, Matthew, and Paulina—as soon as it could be managed. Caroline would probably like to come here and stay with me for a while. It would suit me very well; I would look after her while things were settling themselves."

The other continued to gaze straight before him. "No, Tom," he said at last. "It won't do."

"Why not?"

"For a great many reasons." And Stephen passed his hand wearily over his forehead.

A silence fell and prolonged itself. Abruptly Wentworth got up, and after looking at the barometer, examined the sky again.

"Blowing like hell, isn't it? I hope she isn't going too far."

"No, she won't be going far."

Wentworth faced round; he was now swinging the end of his watch-chain—a sign that he was ill at ease. "Well, to return . . . I can't help suspecting that you're thinking about my health, and in that case I've got something to say. My condition being what it is, it wouldn't be any pleasure to me to have Paulina here. I'd rather she were with you."

"I'm not thinking about your pleasure," returned Stephen gruffly.

There was something so school-boyish in this that Wentworth could not help smiling. "All right. But you've got to think about Paulina's pleasure, haven't you? This is no time for heroics, my dear boy."

Stephen set his jaw. "I am thinking about Paulina. As I have told you before, she has guessed pretty well how things stand with you. And last night she questioned me again. She doesn't want to leave you, Tom. She won't leave you—and she's quite right."

A few moments passed during which the two men studied one another, then with a profound sigh, Wentworth lowered himself down into his chair again.

"Listen, Stephen," he said shortly. "I'm pretty safe to last another three months, so there's plenty of time for Paulina to go to Russia with you and come back. She might even come back alone, if I needed her. She won't have any difficulty in getting out of the country again. For God's sake, take her along with you."

Stephen turned away with a kind of groan. Watching him closely, Wentworth in an even voice went on: " Besides, why the hell can't I die alone if I want to? This is not the time for sentiment but for common sense. I tell you plainly: I don't want Paulina here." And he fumbled in his pocket for a packet of cigarettes.

Stephen continued to stare out over the tree-tops. " Tom," he said dully, " don't let's argue any more. It's no good. Or, if you must, wait till Paulina comes back."

Wentworth put a cigarette between his lips and lit it.

" We had better speak out," he mumbled. " No point now in keeping things back. One of the reasons why I am so insistent is that I'm pretty sure Paulina has ideas in her head. . . ." He looked at Stephen interrogatively. " You know what I mean, don't you? She has a black, superstitious feeling about this parting. I'm certain of it."

" Yes." And Stephen looked down at the ground. " I think you're right."

" On the face of it," Wentworth went on, " there is nothing so very terrible about your having to go back to Russia for a short visit. With luck you ought not to be away for more than three months."

Stephen was silent, then gave an abrupt laugh. " That's true enough," he said.

Wentworth regarded him with distress in his eyes. " It is hard," he said slowly, " when reason and intuition contradict one another."

" My God, it is," said Stephen, looking away. " But, as the future is hidden from us, one must just go ahead. Is there anything else to do, Tom? "

Wentworth paused, then drew a deep breath, and in a voice, the tone of which had suddenly changed, " No! " he said, " you are right. I'll say no more."

After a moment Stephen stirred and got up from his chair. " You've been very good to me, Tom—from the beginning. I'm glad—in a way—for Paulina's sake—that she is to be with you." He turned and went into his room, shutting the door behind him.

.   .   .   .   .

Wentworth remained sitting where he was. He stayed there, motionless, until, lifting his eyes, he saw Paulina step out from under the trees. His gaze was fixed intently upon her as she came towards him, battling against the wind.

" What a turmoil! " she exclaimed, as she threw herself panting into a chair. " How much longer is it going to last? "

Wentworth, still gazing at her with an abstracted air, said nothing.

" Tom! " She leant forward, laughing. " You are in the clouds. What it it? "

" I was thinking."

" Tell me."

" I was thinking that one can't really stand outside life to judge it. The moments when life seems cruel and meaningless are moments when one is affecting—unconsciously, no doubt— to do that. But the intellect is only a little part of the spiritual man; there is nothing good or bad but *feeling* makes it so—not thinking but feeling."

Paulina leant forward and was about to reply when a sudden slant of the wind brought a violent gust, laden with dry leaves, into the veranda, and her voice was lost in the noise of their rustling against the floor and the walls. On all sides, too, a great volume of sound was going up from the tossing, labouring forest. This sound they now listened to without speaking, fascinated by the seemingly human note of anger that it con- tained. But with its change of direction the wind was becoming less violent, and presently with a suddenness that was uncanny all noise died away, and the little house was standing in the midst of a great calm. Almost at once the branches of the trees came to rest; in a few moments not even a leaf was stirring.

" This is terrifying," said Paulina in a whisper, and the next instant she drew back with a start, for lightning had flashed in her eyes.

Thunder followed, and in the deep silence that succeeded it, there came from a distance the thick, enveloping rustle of rain. Louder it grew and louder, and then a few heavy drops struck the veranda roof.

" Now you'll see a real downpour." It was Stephen's voice that sounded behind her and scarcely had he finished speaking before the noise of falling water became deafening, and the landscape was blotted out.

Silent, the three sat watching.

.   .   .   .

Just before dinner Paulina went into the veranda again. In the sky not a cloud was to be seen; the air was fresh with the forest's wetness; a few bright stars had already come out. Looking down, she saw that the house appeared to be standing

in the middle of a small lake, and on the smooth water were
reflected the dark masses of the trees and the luminous evening
sky.

In a few moments Wentworth joined her.

" Tom," she said suddenly. " I wish you would take us to
your glade after dinner. You know, we have never been there;
and this is our last chance."

Wentworth fixed his eyes upon her thoughtfully. " All
right," he said. " We will go."

IV

IT was late when they left the house, but the sky was so bright
with stars that a torch was unnecessary, even under the trees.
Single file they entered the narrow path down to the bayou,
moving through a stillness that was complete, for the drip from
the boughs had now ceased. On reaching the bank they followed it until they came to a boathouse where Wentworth kept
a small boat, and presently they were gliding over the black
water, Paulina sitting beside Wentworth while Stephen rowed.
When they came out from under the trees she looked for the
log upon which she and Stephen had sat together in the early
morning sunshine only three weeks ago, but it was too dark to
see anything clearly except the grassy outline of the banks
where they defined themselves against the sky. " This bayou,"
she thought, " and all the places that I associate with him—
how shall I ever bear to visit them after he is gone?" And in
a moment of sick dread she wanted to flee back to New York.
The great city was without memories; the confused noise of
cities conveyed no message; it was the voice of quiet that she
dreaded, the voice of the quiet earth.

In a little while the boat had again entered the forest, and
now Stephen rowed more slowly, his eyes searching the gloom
of the northern bank. Very soon the glimmer of a narrow
creek became visible; whereupon he stood up, turned the boat
in under the boughs, and began to punt along. The creek was
full, and in places had overflowed its banks so that the rounded
trunks of the trees rose up out of what looked like a vast, sombre
lake. Low on the horizon the moon gave just enough light to
show the way, and thus they proceeded for about a quarter of a
mile, when Wentworth told Stephen to stop.

On their right the ground rose slightly. Here they landed, and Wentworth led the way up a long, wooded slope, at the top of which they came out into an open space. This space, in shape a semi-oval, was surrounded by huge wide-spreading trees, the lower branches of which swept the ground. Each tree, while in line with its neighbour, stood by itself; and the general effect by its symmetry was suggestive of design. Paulina gazed before her with a curiosity into which there gradually crept an element of awe. She understood why Wentworth so often came here. He was drawn by the silence and remoteness of the place, by the stature and grandeur of the trees, and above all by the presiding spirit; for here you felt yourself in the presence of a majestic company.

" The moon will be up soon," said Wentworth. " We shall not have long to wait." With these words he motioned to them to sit down under a tree, the heavy foliage of which had kept the ground dry.

The minutes passed. Seated there with Stephen on one side and Wentworth on the other, Paulina closed her eyes and leant her head back against the massive trunk. " Now is now," she was thinking. " But at this hour to-morrow—what shall I be then?"

The minutes passed; and when she opened her eyes again the forms of the surrounding trees were discernible not only against the sky but against the darkness of the forest that lay behind. At the far end of the oval there appeared to be a gap, but she could not be sure.

Suddenly she felt a pang of intenser anguish; the silence and melancholy of the place, the constant, tormented hooting of the owls—it was more than she could bear. Her hand went out in search of Stephen's and clasped it tightly. " O God, here is Stephen beside me; my hand is clutching his; I touch him, I feel him; but the rim of the moon is pushing up slowly, slowly, from behind the trees; the seconds pass, the minutes pass; and with them he is slipping away from me. These trees stand round like judges; they brood and speak darkly. In them I see Fate; but I want only comfort—only comfort."

" Very soon now,"—it was Wentworth who spoke—" when you see better, you will understand why I like to come here."

In the silence that followed these words they watched the dark tent of the sky gradually filling with light; the moon was rising clear above the level of the forest; and one by one the hooded forms of the communing trees stood forth in smoky silvery brightness. Garmented from head to foot in robes of moss, they took shape in Paulina's vision as patriarchal figures brooding on human destiny. Here was a company of Ancients, and she could even imagine among them, Himself, the Ancient of Days.

Wentworth, too, was lost in contemplation. He was thinking: "How name, how conceive, the spiritual powers that move the suns across the space-abysses, and drive the planets on their circling courses, and rule the tiny and subtle operations of living tissue, and govern the destinies of the human world? How name them? how conceive them? And yet in this endeavour lies the greatness of that creature, Man. The nearness of death seems to confer some spiritual privilege. Sponsored by death I can enter with calm into this silent company."

After a little he heard Stephen give a sigh and mutter as though to himself.

" I was thinking," the young man murmured, " I was thinking that one needs to be reminded. . . . Otherwise one forgets, one becomes unaware . . ."

" What does one forget? "

" That behind all knowledge—all possible knowledge—there is the dark."

For a while no one spoke, then Wentworth said: " One of the oldest of the Vedas runs like this:

' In the beginning Dark-Inert was hid by Dark-Inert. Void by void was overlaid. Will arose therein. The primal seed of Intellect, that was the first. Seed was; All-might was: Intrinsic-Power below, Purpose above. Who knows it aright? Who can here set it forth? Whence was it born? Whence outpoured this came to be, or whether appointed or not, he who is Over-Eye thereof in uttermost Empyrean, he knows indeed, *or knoweth not.*' "

" He knows or knoweth not," echoed Stephen beneath his breath. " And so—*all* is dark; for our very knowledge floats upon darkness."

" Vaughan says: ' There is in God a deep *but dazzling* darkness.' "

Stephen was silent.

" I think," said Wentworth, " all is not *merely* dark."

Again they lost themselves in contemplation, and lost themselves so deeply that they scarcely noticed how the scene was changing. As the moon mounted the sky its globe shrank, its

golden colour faded, its brightness was dimmed. Little by
little the vapours that were thickening the air condensed in
swathes about the feet of the trees, and these, their silvery
radiance dying, melted slowly into the obscurity of the forest
behind. Before long the watery greyness of the sky had
smothered the moon out; a deepening whiteness hid the earth
from sight; and now the three watchers found themselves
isolated in a world that contained only themselves.

"Well," said Wentworth, "it is time to go."

"Oh, not yet," said Paulina, "not quite yet."

"But a moment ago you were shivering. This mist will get
into your bones."

"Not if you come close. Come closer, both of you."

Instead of obeying her Stephen drew back and turned so as
to hold them under his eyes.

"Paulina," he said, "Tom wants you to come to Russia
with me."

Paulina laughed gently, and leaned back against Tom's
shoulder.

"There!" said Stephen, and he drew a deep breath. "You
have your answer, Tom."

Paulina glanced up into Wentworth's face. "Stephen will
be back before very long." Her voice was gentle and confiding.
"You and I, we are going to wait for him here. All that was
settled long ago."

Wentworth, after a pause, inclined his head. "Very well,
but it is not likely that *I* shall see Stephen again. You know
that?"

"Yes—I know. But—here we are together for the moment.
Nothing can rob us of that."

V

EARLY the next day the old taxi-driver—the same man who had
driven Paulina out to the swamp-forest for the first time—saw
her and Stephen drive up to the station, and noticed that there
was luggage in the car. In the last eight years he had passed
her in the street several times, and each time she had recognised
him and smiled. A charming young lady! had been his inward
comment: so when, a little later, he saw her come out of the
station-building, he stepped forward, pleased to take this chance
of offering his services.

But on this occasion she apparently didn't notice him, for she walked straight past without a smile. She was holding herself erect, her face was flushed, her eyes were fixed and unusually bright. After a moment's hesitation he hurried after her and took a few steps by her side; but still she seemed not to notice him; so at last he went so far as to touch her lightly on the arm. " Lady . . ." he said.

She glanced round, stopped, and to his relief the queer look on her face disappeared. " Oh, it's you! "

" Yes. I thought maybe . . ."

His sentence died away because, rather disconcertingly, her eyes had immediately become remote again. " Maybe you'd like a drive," he resumed in a louder voice. " There was a place you wanted to get to once. . . . Do you remember, lady? I found it for you all right. And I guess I could take you right back there now, if you wanted to go."

" Yes," said Paulina. " I do."

He had not expected this; but, after another moment of perplexity, he steered her towards his car, chatting rather jerkily as he went. When she had got in he gave her another look and said: " Drive you to the *hotel*, lady? " And in order to reach her across the distance that seemed to lie between them he repeated: " To the hotel, lady? Drive you to the hotel? "

" No," she replied. " No. Not to the hotel. To—that place."

Well; there was nothing more to be said. So he got into his seat and drove off.

As they were passing the cemetery Paulina leaned forward and gazed at it intently. It was still early morning; the sunlight in the willows that bordered the canal made a pale green rain, the shadows of the cypresses lay long and dark across the white tombs. " Yes," she thought, " it is beautiful—beautiful."

A little later the car drew up at the side of the road.

" This is the place, ain't it? " The old man was looking round at her with a grin.

" It is. And how clever of you to remember! "

He came round and opened the door. " You want me to wait, lady? "

" No. Don't wait." And then, as he looked puzzled, she added: " I live here."

He was still puzzled, but her manner made him feel sure that she knew what she was about. " Goodbye," she said with a smile.

" Goodbye, lady."

For as long as she remained in sight he watched her, his own smile lingering upon his face. Then with a little shake of the head he got back into his seat and drove off.

Slowly Paulina walked down the track. With one part of her mind she was conscious of the softness of the air, the profound silence, and the slant of the sunlight through the tall, yellow grasses by the wayside. But her spirit was absent. Just before the train had started there had been a moment when Stephen had turned to her, and she had seen upon his face a look at which something within her had said: " On this you can live. After this, surely, you need not ask for anything more. Remember this! Cling to this!" And in great pride and humility—and also with wonder at the beauty of what she had seen—she had stood there watching the train go out, almost forgetting to wave her hand or to smile.

And now, as she walked slowly along under the pale lofty sky, with the grey-bearded trees shimmering in the distance, this world, at once intensely familiar and intensely strange, seemed, like a friend, to have knowledge of what was in her heart. Its quiet was for her—that she might dwell upon the inward vision that her heart contained.

.   .   .

For about a fortnight after Stephen's departure she remained in a kind of trance. The forest, now in full leaf, was so dense and secret that she had only to take a few steps outside the clearing to feel herself remote; and into this remoteness she retired, sitting for long hours with her back against the trunk of a tree and staring before her, until she became a creature to whom the present and the future were nothing, and the past merely the substance out of which dreams were to be distilled. But little by little, as time went on, the nature of her dreams changed, and she would also sink into a state in which she felt as though she were sharing with all Nature in a deep contentment which was proper to the bare condition of existing.

One day she spoke about this to Wentworth, who smiled and said: " Yes, I know what you mean."

" But what does it mean?"

" Ah! That I do not know. And yet in all times and among all peoples it has been the same. There is—for those who can find it—a secret pool of beatitude beneath the crust of the external world." He paused. " And complete self-identification with Nature seems to bring an equal bliss."

" Bliss? " Paulina repeated thoughtfully. " Beatitude? "

" Yes, they are there. But how this comes to be, or what it means . . ."

However, after this conversation, instead of encouraging her to go forward on this path, he was, she could see, not a little troubled on her account. He would say rather testily: " My dear child, you must remember that you are still young. You and Stephen both have more than half a lifetime before you. You have got to *live* and *rejoice*."

Of Stephen they talked very little; and as a rule only when his letters arrived. On these occasions Wentworth always spoke as if he were confident that Stephen would soon be back. Letters were fairly frequent until Stephen reached the Russian frontier; after that they not only became infrequent but were much less satisfying, for they contained nothing that could not pass beneath a censor's eye. Paulina had the hopes that Stephen would find a means of smuggling letters—*real* letters— out of the country, and for these she waited with an anxiety that was with her all the time. But days and weeks passed and no such letters came.

Fear lay at the back of her mind; one layer of her being was swept by storms of grief; there were moments when her outward calm seemed to her to be a mockery and a sham.

.   .   .   .   .

Meanwhile Spring had turned into Summer, and a damp tropical heat, of which she had had no previous experience, added to her sense of being suspended in a region outside the real world. She spent the still, stagnant days indoors sunk in a stupor that lifted only with the fall of night. Then in an air bright with fire-flies and heavy with the smell of the dewy forest she would awake to an intense, if still remote activity of mind. She felt far away from everything—even herself.

In this midsummer heat hardly a night passed without Wentworth's stealing out of the house; and when the moon was full he would often be absent for several hours. Paulina did not find it hard to guess where he went; but she had no wish to accompany him, nor did he ever suggest it.

Not infrequently, however, seized with restlessness and even with anxiety, she would get up from her bed and sit on the veranda-steps, awaiting his return. Then, when he appeared, he would stand leaning against the railings at her side, and sometimes they would talk, but more often they were silent.

In the course of these nocturnal conversations a more and

more vivid sense of the spiritual world as he conceived it gained possession of her mind; and this new vision brought her peace, but a peace that was broken—especially at first—by moments when she slipped into uncertainty, and even into a kind of terror. Then it seemed to her that either Wentworth was touched with insanity or that the rest of the world was mad. The *unawareness* of most people made children of them; they were children playing with brittle toys, children running hither and thither on a thin and brittle surface through which, one and all, they needs must break at last—to fall, after a profitless life, into an empty death. Reality, significant and dark, stretched above them and beneath them, and they regarded it not.

For some time past Wentworth had been steadily losing strength; she had seen him changing. Hardly a week went by without his being stricken down by severe pain, and for several days after each attack he would lie on his bed unable to move from exhaustion, and waiting impatiently for sufficient strength to return to enable him to do what he most cared to do—wander about the forest at night. The pain he bore with stoicism, but in his subsequent exhaustion he was irritable. He frequently gave Paulina the sense that almost anyone else's ministrations would have pleased him better than hers.

VI

THERE came a night in August when, after hearing him leave the house, she was seized with an anxiety which gradually became more acute than any she had known before. And yet was it actually anxiety that possessed her? No, it was rather a sense of crisis—the feeling that for her as well as for him a culmination had been reached. She saw that a decision had been taking shape in her mind; and now it stood there full-formed; and she felt the necessity of communicating it to Wentworth because by so doing she would be setting the seal upon her resolve.

After a while she got up and went out on to the veranda. High overhead the full moon shone down from an almost cloudless sky. " He has gone to the glade," she thought, and sat down on the steps, prepared to wait for a long time.

An hour went by, then another. She fell into a dream, so that it was with a start that she lifted her head at last to see him step out from under the trees. A tall pale figure—hair, face, and thin tropical suit all alike grey in the moonlight—he came towards her across the clearing, and she noticed at once that he was bearing himself more vigorously than usual.

" It has been a good night," he said.

His voice had an exultant ring, and while she continued to look up at him he went on: " Paulina, I wish I could tell you. . . . How I wish I could tell you! But these things are incommunicable."

Leaning against the post in his accustomed place, he kept silence for some time, then said: " There is a deep-seated thrill that is not of the flesh, nor of the mind, but of the spirit."

Paulina's lips parted for speech, but he was looking up into the sky, and she realized that he had lost awareness of her presence.

" Excitement suffused with awe, with peace, with joy! " He seemed to be talking as much to himself as to her. " There is no illusory sense of understanding—only the profound realization that Mystery *is*."

And again, after a pause, he went on: " It comes and then it goes; it is not possible that it should last long. But to-night it lasted long enough, and the descent was not abrupt. Gradually I emerged out of that heaven into the spaces of this starry sky. Gradually I sank down towards the earth; I saw it sailing beneath me. All then became familiar and very dear to my heart. I knew where I was. It was my home. I saw and felt the beauty of earth as never before."

He lowered his head and as his eyes wandered over the familiar outlines of the trees, Paulina's gaze automatically followed his. She thought: " Wherever I live, and whenever I die . . ."

Wentworth's voice again came to her, and it seemed far away. " But that was not all. My dear child, for the first time in my life I saw Man through the eyes of God. I saw the exquisite beauty that springs—and can only spring—from the relation between creature and Creator. To Man there is given the privilege of worship—that I have known and felt for a long time. But to-night I saw Man as he stands in the vision of compassionate God. Raised very little above the beasts of the field, feeble of mind, sickly in body, oppressed by circumstances, blind of spirit; blackly and inescapably overshadowed by old age, disease and death, Man yet *struggles hard*. Consider the standards that he sets himself—his ideals of courage, of generosity, of endurance! Consider not only Man's disinterested devotion to truth, but his passion for nobility, his restless search after greatness. Consider that unconquerable fastidiousness which forces him to toil, always to toil, in order to bring the poor, flesh-bound, witless creature that he is a little nearer to what he wishes to be."

Paulina motioned to Wentworth to seat himself beside her, for quite suddenly his face had shown signs of extreme weariness.

He complied, then added after a minute: "The fact that I have seen what I have seen shows, I think, that my end must be near.—I am thankful for my sake as well as yours."

She answered: "I am glad you have had this, Tom. You look happy."

Wentworth smiled. "Happy! Yes, I am."

A long silence rested upon them before anything more was said; and when at last Paulina spoke her voice was hesitating and low. "I, too, want to tell you something. Thinking about Stephen and the future, I have come to feel that I oughtn't to be another reason for his giving up Russia. He believes—and I know you do too—that a new civilisation, a better life, are being attempted there. And that being his belief . . ."

"He and I," said Wentworth, "are both convinced that in the history of this world there are moments when men must make a change, must strike out upon a new path. I believe that there are successive dispensations, and that what is the right rule of life in one period may become the wrong one in the next. The same inspiration, the same spiritual force, is at work; but, when the hour comes, a change is enjoined. That the new spirit should appear materialistic—should indeed believe itself to be materialistic—must not confuse you. The explanation is this: the new spirit is in arms against a social order that continues to fly the banner of idealism after it has lost the right to do so. Inspiration is now on the other side. If you look back, you will see that the same thing has happened before. Think of the resistance of civilized Paganism to Christianity! Such changes often seem retrograde and cruel—especially when, as to-day, many good men are without the vision to transfer their allegiance."

"Yes," said Paulina, "I think you and Stephen are probably right. In any case, Stephen, feeling as he does, ought not to step back into the old life, nor ought I to be another inducement. What I must do—later on—is to join him in Russia. I believe I could make his daily life out there quite endurable. He himself has never denied it. What do you think, Tom?"

Wentworth turned his head away. "My dear, that is a question which you—and you alone . . ."

" But say something to me—please ! "

Wentworth gave a sigh. " The new civilization misunder-
stands itself and its own spirit, and yet—and yet—the force of
life that is carrying it along testifies for it. Regeneration is
there."

" Well, then . . ? "

Wentworth got up and upon his face Paulina saw a look of
great sadness. " My dear," he said, as he climbed wearily up
the steps, " I'm afraid you are right."

.   .   .   .   .

The weeks that followed this conversation were not unlike
those that had gone before. Wentworth's exhaustion was increasing, but increasing slowly, and every day he came to depend
on Paulina a little more. His midnight wanderings ceased, and
for this she was thankful; but one night, about a month later,
she woke with a start to hear him making his way softly and
cautiously down the veranda-steps. After a few minutes of
agonised indecision she got up and went out. Standing in the
middle of the clearing she listened, looking anxiously in every
direction. She ran a little way down the path to the bayou,
but he was not to be seen or heard. Then suddenly another
idea came into her mind: she went to see if he was sitting on
his log, and there she found him.

He had heard her coming, and in the broken moonlight under
the trees she saw his face turned towards her, but his expression
was indecipherable. Not daring to come closer she stood
and looked at him.

It was in a trembling voice that she said at last: " Tom,
please promise me this . . . Promise that you won't
attempt——"

" I can't say," he replied; and then added more gently.
" You needn't worry, my dear. I know I haven't the strength
to get there."

The next day Paulina wrote to Stephen to say that Wentworth's death was very near, and that she would start for Russia
immediately after it. She had already written fully to prepare
him for this decision, but always with difficulty, for she was
possessed by a deep-seated conviction that the course of her
destiny and Stephen's had already been taken out of their hands.

And then came a night when she had a strange dream. She
had lain down to sleep with door and window open, and the
moonlight streaming into her room. She was lying there, as
she thought, meditating, when suddenly it seemed to her that

Stephen was coming up on to the veranda; she heard his footsteps quite plainly; and the next moment he walked in. She was not in the least astonished at seeing him; nor was there in her mind any memory of his having been away. She sat up in bed and looked at him enquiringly, and he said: "Come! I am going to take you to Tom." At once she knew that Tom was dead; so she got up, put on her dressing-gown and went with Stephen. He took her by the hand—and at this she was a little surprised, for it was not a thing that he often did—and together they went down the veranda towards Tom's room. But the veranda stretched on and on, and they went forward hand in hand for a period that was not to be measured in hours, or days, or years. She went on and on with a deep and peaceful sense of security; she felt faith in the midst of mystery, secure in the feeling that Stephen was there, and that ultimately Tom would be reached.

And it was with this same feeling upon her that she woke.

Her room was cold and grey; there was no moonlight, but a misty dawn was breaking. After a moment she got up, put on her dressing-gown, and went along the veranda into Tom's room. Her first glance confirmed her in the knowledge that he was dead. His jaw had dropped, his eyes were staring, but his hands folded upon his chest showed that he had died peacefully.

Two days later the burial took place in the cemetery which she had passed so often during the last eight years. In the interval she had been in a state of calm which she herself could not understand, for this strange calm floated upon suspense. Deep in her heart she felt: "This is not all. This is not all. We live in a present that is more than half hidden from us. Not our future alone but our present contains that which we do not know."

A letter from Stephen was now overdue, and she was waiting. Ever since her dream she had been living in the conviction that Stephen had communicated with her, and this conviction was fortified by a recurrent sense of his presence. In the bright sunlight of the clearing he moved, and this feeling of his nearness inspired her with both terror and reassurance. But at other times her frame of mind was quite different; in imagination she would dwell upon the details of her approaching meeting with Stephen and upon the life that lay before them. In these pictures Matthew took an important place. "Before very long

I shall actually be seeing him," she thought. "I wonder if he will like me."

On a dull and misty afternoon, the last before her journey, she was standing in the veranda when the mulatto girl came and handed her a letter. It had a Russian stamp, but the handwriting was not Stephen's, and it was addressed to Wentworth. She opened it. The matron of the hospital at Kharkov announced that both Stephen and Caroline had died of typhus. Matthew had escaped the illness and was well.

Paulina folded the letter carefully and put it back into the envelope; then she walked quickly into her room and went on with her packing. In the deathly blankness of her mind one thought repeated itself; to one thought she clung desperately: "Matthew is still alive." She packed with automatic speed and energy: in half an hour's time the room was as bare as when she had first entered it.

Going out on to the veranda again, she stood and looked into the grey of the misty forest. The mist was gathering; the light was fading, but the motionless trees still stood forth in the shapes that she knew so well. After a while she went down the steps, took the little path to the bayou, and presently found herself sitting upon the log where she and Stephen had sat together on that morning four months ago. The bayou was now surrounded by darkness; already the wide marshes on either side were featureless and dim. That straight pathway of water gathered and held upon its melancholy stillness all the last lights of the cloudy sky.